Hollar

Book 4

Screaming Mimi

Published in the United States of American in the year 2021;

The right of the Authors Name to be identified as the Author of the Work has been asserted by them in accordance with The Copyright, Designs and Patent Act of 1988.

Published by: Screaming Mimi

Cover art by: SC Photo – Shelton Cole

Edited by: Jodi Cowan

Interior formatting and design by: Screaming Mimi & Shelton Cole

Copyright 2021 © Screaming Mimi

Language: English

ISBN-13: 9798719453422

Thank You

To my cover models Saibra Sorensen and Max OB, you two gave me the perfect muses for Bella and Holland. Shelton Cole thank you for this completely epic book cover. To my editor Jodi Cowan, thank you for making my words sound better. To my Screamers, who have waited what seems like forever for this book, thank you for your patience. As always thank you to my scream making hubby who helps with all my research, and I do mean ALL my research.

WARNING!!

This book is for adults only. It deals with strong situations that could cause triggers for some individuals. Please be advised that if you have a weak constitution you should not go any further. You've been warned.

Chapter One

Approximately One Year Ago

HOLLAND

I made my way over to the petite redhead that looked like she was trying to curl herself into her own body when it happened. The one person I never thought I'd see again, my mother. She was thinner and older, but it was definitely her. I was in such a state of shock at seeing her; it took me a moment to take in all of her. Her hair was a different shade of blonde that looked like it hadn't been washed in a few days at least, lying limp against her shoulders. Dark thick make-up coated her face, and it reminded me of a mask. She was wearing a jean mini skirt that looked to be two sizes too small and a halter-top that barely covered anything.

"Are you listening to me dumbass? I said how the hell am I supposed to make money if you take all my girls?" She didn't recognize me, not even a little, it was like a stab to the little boy who lived inside my heart. I'm too shocked to even respond. The whimpers of the redheaded girl caught my attention, causing me to glance her way again.

"You like her? You want her? I can make that happen; me, no one else." I looked back at the woman who gave birth to me and couldn't believe the words that were coming out of her mouth. The girl eyed me for a minute before ducking her head back inside her cocoon. She started rocking back and forth and I could hear sounds of crying emanating from her. Choosing to ignore my mother, I strode over to the girl to make sure she was all right; sitting down close enough for us to talk, but far enough away not to spook her.

"Hey, my name is Holland. What's yours?" She shook her head and if it was possible, she seemed to burrow further into herself.

"Hey, I'm not going to hurt you. I'm a police officer, I'm here to help." She peeked at me from between the arms she had crossed over her knees.

"You're with those bikers, you aren't a cop, try another lie." Woah, this kid had spunk, and she was definitely still a kid. Maybe sixteen or seventeen, I couldn't be sure, but she was definitely not like the rest of the prostitutes we rounded up. I reached into my back pocket and pulled out my badge.

"Here, look. Go on take it." She tentatively reached out her hand and snatched my badge before yanking her hand back.

"Holy shit! You are a cop. What the fuck are you doing here with all these bikers?" Her voice raised an octave and she unfurled herself a little.

"Those bikers are my buddies, my real family, they needed some help, it's that simple." I shrugged like that explained it all, but she didn't look convinced. It was that simple for me, they were my family even if I wasn't a part of the club; they were my family.

"Seriously, how did a cop get to be buddies with bikers. You dirty?" She eyed me with suspicion, and I laughed.

"No, definitely not. Maybe a little on the grey side of the law but definitely not the dirty side. What about you kid, how did you get involved with this riffraff?" She looked down at my badge rubbing it with her thumb, deep in thought.

"Doesn't matter." She shrugged looking lost. "Am I going to be arrested or something?"

"Do you have anyone you can call to come pick you up?" She shook her head.

"Your parents?" She shook her head.

"Aunts? Uncles? Cousins twice removed?" She continued to shake her head no.

"Come on kid you gotta have someone out there looking for you. Someone who gives a shit." No way there wasn't at least someone out there that cared about her.

"Who do you think sold me?" She jumped up and threw my badge at me, anger pouring off her.

"My own fucking parents that's who. They needed money for drugs, I was the payment. This is my life now." Tears started streaming down her face as she crumbled to the ground. What the fuck was wrong with people? First Bliss's dad and his bullshit and now this kid's parents. It made me want to hunt these fuckers down and give them my own brand of justice.

"What's your name kid? I can't keep calling you kid." I wanted to give her a hug or some kind of comfort but I knew from being around Bliss that wasn't something I could do. She needed to know I was safe not some asshole trying to cop a feel.

"Crimson, Crimson Reed." I blinked at her, because no fucking way was that her real name.

"I've had the red hair since birth, apparently my parents thought my name should match. I know it sounds like a stripper name, which considering what I've been doing would be better than my current occupation." I flinch remembering where I found her, in a den of prostitution.

"How old are you Crimson? And don't lie because I know damn well you aren't an adult." She looked like she was nervous or afraid that if she told me her age she'd be going to jail or juvie or something equally horrible.

"I'm not going into foster care, or any other bullshit thing you're thinking about. I'm old enough to take care of myself, besides I learned a lot of skills working for these guys. I'm sure I can make money to support myself." I cringed to think about the skills she was talking about. My own sisters were barely older than she was, if anyone ever touched them without their consent, I don't know what I'd do. Probably be on trial for murder I'm pretty sure.

"Who said anything about foster care? I'm simply asking friendly questions to get to know you, that's all. How long have you been with these assholes anyway?" Even if she was eighteen, she was barely eighteen but I highly doubted that.

"You ask a lot of questions, questions I'm pretty sure you don't really want the answers to." I shrugged at her in response and waited.

"Fine, I'm seventeen, there you satisfied Mr. Hot Cop." I raised an eyebrow at the hot cop reference; I did not need her to be thinking of me in that way at all. I definitely wasn't thinking about her in that way, she reminded me of my sisters at her age for that shit.

"Don't act like you don't know you're hot." She sighed.

"I've been here for six months, but they didn't make me start...you know until last month. Some dude paid big bucks to pop my cherry, then I was only given to "special clients", their words not mine." I rubbed my hand over my face, and wanted to find her parents and bash their fucking brains in.

"So, you want some of this or what? Don't look at me like I've offended you, I've had guys way older than you already, at least you're hot. There are beds inside, we can..." It was my turn to jump up and glare down at her. I put my hands out to stop her from going any further in her explanation of what we could do.

"Woah! Stop, just stop right there. I'm trying to help you, nothing more. Haven't you ever had someone that only wanted to help you because they could? Someone you could depend on, that took care of you?" Someone, somewhere in her life had to have had this kid's back. Life couldn't be so cruel as to give her no one.

"Yeah, my sister Bella; but she ran out and I haven't heard from her since. So, I guess I couldn't even depend on her. She became some guy's old lady in some biker gang and never looked back. She was smart, she saw a chance to get the fuck out and she took it. I wish I had done the same thing." I cringed thinking that if her sister thought that was her only way out. Not all motorcycle clubs were like Bart's, some were full of sick twisted bastards. Suddenly I felt a need to protect them both from people like that.

"How old was she when she left?" Maybe if I got enough information, I could find her sister and reunite them. This kid deserves someone to give a shit about her.

"You ask a lot of questions." She huffed before releasing her legs she'd been holding onto for dear life the last half hour and shifting closer to me.

"Bella packed her shit in the middle of the night a few months before I was sold to these assholes. Birthdays weren't exactly celebrated in our house, but she's three years older than I am. Any other questions you feel like getting off your chest Mr. Hot Cop?" She inched closer to me and put her fingernail against my chest. I, in return, stood up and put distance between us.

"You afraid of me Mr. Hot Cop? I promise I don't bite, well unless you want me to." Putting my hands up in front of myself to ward her off, I stepped back.

"Crimson, you need to stop. Whatever you think is going to happen, isn't going to happen. I'm only trying to help you out, that's all, I don't want anything from you." I ran my hand through my hair wanting to strangle the fuckers who had done this to her.

"I want to help you too Mr. Hot Cop, I know how to help you out real good." Shaking my head at her, I stood my ground. Anger flashed in her eyes when she realized her "charms" weren't working on me.

"Oh please, you're a man, eventually you'll cave. They all want to act like they don't want to but, in the end, they always take what they want. You aren't any better than all the men that came before you. Hell, even some of them promised to get me out of there, take me somewhere safe, it was all lies. All men do is lie." Tears were streaming down her face and I resisted the urge to comfort her, I knew if I did, she'd get the wrong idea again. Damn my mother, damn Jack Finch and his morally bankrupt fucking sick twisted mind. This girl should be in school daydreaming about her first kiss, not this, definitely not this. How was I going to convince her I was different? I looked down at my shoes wondering if by some miracle they would have the answer, alas they did not.

"Look Crimson, men can definitely be assholes, I won't even try to deny that, but I want nothing from you but to help you. That's all, if you don't want my help I'll leave, and you can go about your life." Deep down I didn't want to walk away from this girl, she needed someone to give a damn about her, and right now I was it. But if she could only see me as a man who wanted her for her body then I couldn't help her.

"NO! Please, Holland, don't go." She grabbed onto my arm before I could pull it back but let go quickly.

"I'm sorry, I'm a bitch, I know this. No one has ever...you know given a shit other than my sister. But it doesn't even feel like she gave a shit in the end. I mean she ran off without even trying to take me with her, I couldn't have meant that much to her." She shrugged before wrapping her arms around her middle.

"You're not a bitch Crimson, people were assholes to you, and you've been through some heavy shit. But this," I pointed back and forth between us, "this is just friendship I'm offering with no strings attached to it. I help you out, you get to move on with your life, and hopefully, put this shit behind you. Deal?" I reached my hand out to shake on it and she reluctantly took it.

"So how does this work, you helping me out. You aren't turning me into child services, are you? You said you wouldn't." If I didn't know better, I'd swear I was looking at a younger version of Bliss. I've lost my mind thinking I can fix the world and their problems.

"Well for starters you're going to come live with me." Her eyes lit up like a Christmas tree right before they narrowed at me with suspicion.

"Don't give me that look, I have a couple of spare rooms. You will live in one of them. We will also figure out a way to get you enrolled in school or take a GED test. Whichever you prefer, and then you will get a job. But most importantly you are going to start seeing a therapist." Now she gave me a slightly outraged look before giving me a quick nod.

"Fine Mr. Hot Cop, lead the way, I'm all yours." She giggled, like she was actually a teenage girl, and not like a woman trying to be seductive.

"Very funny short stuff. You got any shit back there you want to go grab, if not this whole place is going up in flames shortly." She shook her head and we headed to my truck. I had no idea why I was doing this, what made me take on this responsibility, but there was something driving me to protect her at all cost, even at the cost of my sanity.

Chapter Two

HOLLAND

I've been searching for the last two months for
Crimson's sister, with no luck so far. It's like she disappeared
off the face of the planet and I feared the worst. Crimson, for
the most part, has kept up her end of the bargain. She got her
GED, found a job at the local bar as a waitress, and started
seeing a therapist. We've gotten into a routine, I work during
the day while she cleans the house and makes dinner every
night, then I drop her off at work after dinner. I can tell she's
thinking of us as more than roommates, I've tried to nip that
in the bud, because all I feel for her is brotherly affection.

I'm just getting ready for work when I hear the
rumbling sounds of a motorcycle pulling into my drive.
Thinking it's either Bart or Matty, I swing open the front
door with a grin on my face. I'm stopped short as I take in the
tricked out blue bagger sitting in my driveway with the

sexiest woman, I've ever seen pulling off her helmet. She's wearing leather pants that hugged her legs and thighs like they were a second skin giving me the perfect view of a luscious ass. As she slid off the bike, she removed her sunglasses and glared up at me with scorn in her eyes. I had no idea who the fuck this woman was, but I'd pissed her off somehow. She unzipped her leather jacket to reveal a skintight tank that barely contained her full breasts.

"Are you Holland?" She ground out as she stomped her way up the walkway.

"Hey, eyes up here asshole, I said are you Holland?" I must have been staring at her chest; in my defense those things needed their own zip code, because she snapped her fingers to get my attention. If my sisters or Dad saw me right now, I'd be getting an ass chewing from hell. Finally finding my voice, I stood a little straighter and focused on her face.

"Yeah, I'm Holland. The real question is who are you?" I grin at her trying to diffuse whatever anger she has for me.

"You have something that belongs to me." She went to push her way past me, but I grabbed onto her upper arm before she could make it too far.

"Let go of me asshole before I put a bullet in that pretty little head of yours." I was shocked, first by the amount of vehemence behind her words, and second because she thought I had a pretty head.

"So you think I'm pretty?" How had I gone from mature, grown ass, police officer, to fifteen-year-old dork staring at the pretty girl in the last five minutes, I'm not sure. She growled at me, before yanking her arm out of my grip and stomping into my house.

"Where is she? I swear if you touched her, I don't care if you are a cop I'll bury you in your own backyard." I was beginning to think she was some crazy woman with the way she was talking until she started searching the house yelling.

"Crimson! Crimson, are you in here? Crimson, honey I'm here to rescue you." Holy fucking batshit, batballs, Batman, this was Crimson's sister, Bella. She spun around on me, catching me ogling her ass, I don't know what the hell has gotten into me at this point. This is not who I am, I'm the good guy, the solid guy, the one everyone thinks is gay because I don't ogle or hit on women. Thrusting her finger at my chest, she got right in my face.

"Where the fuck is my sister asswipe?" Before I can answer, Crimson's squeals of excitement are coming from down the hallway.

"Bella! Bella, is that really you? Oh my GOD!" Crimson came barreling down the hallway and ran into her sister.

"You're here, you're really here. You found me!" Crimson hung onto Bella like she was the life preserver, and her ship was going down.

"Hey peanut, of course I found you." Bella suddenly got very quiet as she stroked Crimson's hair and hugged her close. I walked into the kitchen to make breakfast, giving them a moment. Their voices were barely above a whisper as they sat on my couch chattering to each other. I stayed quiet as I made enough breakfast for all of us. I was so focused on giving them privacy that I didn't hear Bella when she snuck up behind me.

"So." I flinch slightly and turn around to find her leaning against the other counter. Her right hand is on the counter, the heel of her boot against the floor where she is rolling in back and forth on the heel. All the badass biker bitch from before seems to have vanished as she looks down at her boots with remorse.

"Look, about what I said outside…" I hold my hand to stop her with the spatula still in it.

"We can talk after I get finished with these eggs, go ahead and have a seat." I jerk my chin to the small four-person kitchen table and chair set sitting in my dining room. The cabin I live in was originally only meant for weekends and summers, but when my dad gave it to me, I decided I liked living out in no man's land and made it home.

"You're seriously making breakfast? You, Holland, are not at all what I expected when I came here." She smiled as she slowly made her way over to the table and chairs.

"I'm not sure if I should be offended or happy about that statement. I take it you're going to take Crimson with you when you leave." It's not a question, because I already know by the sounds coming from Crimson's room she's probably packing up.

"I've been looking for you since…" I wasn't sure how much Crimson wanted to tell her or had told her, and I wasn't about to reveal more than she was ready to, even if it was her sister.

"Since you rescued her from those sick fuckballs, yeah thanks for that by the way." She didn't look up at me, instead she fiddled with her nail polish.

"It should have been me; did she tell you that? I thought she was safe until she was old enough at least. They waited until I was eighteen, I thought they would do the same with Crimson, I was wrong. She paid for my ignorance, my belief, and now I'll spend the rest of my life making that up to her." Bella sounded like she had the weight of the world resting on her shoulders, and there was something deep inside me that wanted to help her with that burden.

"What they did is on them, not on you, and not on Crimson. Don't put that on yourself, you are barely an adult, they were your parents, both of you should have been safe with them. They fucked up, not you." Her shoulders seem to relax just a little as I bring the plates of food over to the table.

"She said you were a good guy, Crimson did, and I didn't want to believe her. Most men I've met aren't good decent men when it comes to young girls, if you know what I mean. But you took her in, helped her grow, even tried to find me. Which you did, by the way, that's why I'm here." Sitting down I looked at her in confusion, I was pretty sure she'd found me not the other way around.

"A few weeks ago, you made contact with a crew that is in my territory, they in return contacted me, and poof I'm here." Wait, did she just say her territory?

"Your territory? I thought you were some guy's old lady, that's what Crimson told me." I had a feeling there was more to this woman than meets the eye, just based off of the epic bike sitting outside in my drive. If she was an old lady, her old man would have brought her here, no way he'd let her go alone.

"Yeah, that's a long story, and not one I can tell a cop." She clipped out before loading her plate up and diving into breakfast. Crimson came out with her bag packed up, looking at me sheepishly.

"Holland, I know you're going to be lonely without me, but I'm going with my sister." Crimson thrust her chin out and held her head up high. She'd come a long way from the girl who couldn't look me in the eyes, she was more confident and self-assured. It made me smile.

"You planning on skipping out on work without telling them you're leaving?" Her face fell and I almost regretted mentioning it to her. She should go with her sister, she deserved to go and be happy. But there was a part of me that wanted to keep them here just a little longer.

"Shit, I totally forgot. Bell I can't just leave them in the lurch like that. Think you can stick around until after my shift." Crimson looked nervous asking her sister to wait for her, like she'd leave her if she didn't come with her right that second. Bella looked like she was ready to say no, but then her face softened.

"Sure, kid we can wait, if Holland here doesn't mind putting me up for the night." Inside I gave myself a fist bump for that going smoothly. Crimson would get a chance to say goodbye to the friends she'd made at work. It had nothing to do with wanting to spend more time with Bella, at least that's what I told myself.

"Good that's settled, now eat before I leave. I only have a few more minutes before I have to get to work. I'll be home the usual time, if you want you can order pizza instead of cooking." There was a part of me that would miss having her around, she reminded me of my sisters, and I missed them like crazy since they started college.

"You sure you're alright with me hanging around your place without you being here. I could rob you blind and you wouldn't be here to stop me." Bella got a little sassy as I started cleaning up my plate and the breakfast dishes. It was like she was trying to get under my skin, but I wasn't going to let her.

"I don't have much worth stealing, ask Crimson." I nod toward her sister who is still sitting at the table watching our exchange.

"Yeah, he totally doesn't, even the motorcycle in his garage doesn't start." I give her my best, how dare you look. "Well, it's true, don't give me that look."

"I'm working on it, Sassy McSasspants. Rebuilds take time." I say defensively and she giggles at the table.

"Yeah, they take time, not centuries, dude. And that nickname shit is why people think you're gay. The point is it's worthless just like most of the junk in this place. Don't let Bella scare you Holls she won't steal anything I'll make sure of it." Bella looks shocked at our banter back and forth.

"People think you're gay?" Bella asked while giving me the once over.

"I'm not gay, not that there is anything wrong with being gay, but I like women. We've gone over this Crimson. I helped raise my sisters, I can't help it if some of their personalities rubbed off on me." I look at the clock and if I don't get out of there, I'm going to be late.

"Look, I'm trusting you to behave while I'm at work, which I have to get to like ten minutes ago." I grabbed my lunch out of the fridge and high-tailed it out the door before I could be embarrassed any more.

Chapter Three

BELLA

Holland was nothing like I thought he'd be. When I heard my sister was with a cop my mind automatically thought he was using her. In my experience, men didn't do things for you without there being a price to be paid. Holland wasn't like any of the men I'd ever dealt with. He cared about my sister like she was his own. I won't lie, it made me slightly envious of her.

"He's pretty awesome, isn't he?" Crimson asked, startling me from my musings. I shrugged my shoulder in a noncommittal way.

"Oh, don't give me that shrug missy, you know he's hot. I know he's hot, so I know you know he's hot. I've been trying to tempt him since day one with no luck." I wanted to fucking kill our parents, and maybe I would if I ever found them for putting her into the position, she'd been in.

"You shouldn't be trying to tempt a grown ass man, especially a cop that's letting you live with him for free. Were you trying to get kicked out, because that's how you get kicked out?" Crimson shook her head laughing.

"First of all, I've been with men much older than him. Second, Holland isn't like that Bell, he'd never kick me out because I was being a dumbass. He actually gives a shit about me. Like really gives a shit. I told you he had requirements for me living here, and not the kind of requirements that I need to be on my knees or on my back either. I had to get my GED, get a job, and help around the house. He's the genuine article sis, a good man." I still found it hard to believe that a man would take in a teenage girl who by all accounts was a prostitute when he found her without wanting something in return.

There was no mistaking the man was fine; he had this clean-cut thing going for him. Something I didn't usually go for, because bad boys were usually my thing. My last bad boy got me my freedom from my parents, not that he turned out to be much better, but at least I got away from them. Holland just had this aura about him that screamed good guy though, but without looking like a weakling. No, it was obvious that man had some seriously restrained power behind him. I briefly wondered how much of that restrained power would come out in the bedroom.

"Yeah whatever, you found yourself a genuine white knight, he even comes with a shield." We both laughed. Crimson got up and started cleaning her dishes and tidying up.

"Wow, look at you so domesticated, he's got you trained up right." Crimson gave me a frown like I'd offended her. I meant it as a joke, but she didn't seem to find it funny.

"He taught me that taking pride in where you stay makes you want to take pride in yourself and the things you do. My therapist taught me that cluttered surroundings can lead to cluttered minds. And cluttered minds can bring on the bad thoughts I have sometimes." That's when I realized that the sister, I left wasn't the sister I found. She'd grown, she'd lived through hell, and come out the other end better for it. Instead of letting what happened break her, she'd had support that let her grow from it.

"Holy shit Crim, that's some deep shit right there. I'm so fucking proud of you, you know that right. I thought when I got here, I'd find some frightened girl being abused by some fat cop. Instead, you've blossomed into a strong independent woman." I pulled her into a crushing hug, holding back the tears that threatened to flow.

"Who lives with a hot cop, don't forget about the hot cop thing. I mean did you see his ass, girl you could bounce a quarter off of it. Not that he'd ever let me, but damn." She made grabby hands like she was trying to grab his ass and I shook my head at her.

"You're incorrigible, you know that. But you're right he's hot." We giggled like schoolgirls talking about our first crush.

I started thinking of the ways I could thank Holland for everything he'd done for Crimson. Naughty ways. Ways to make his back arch and his toes to curl. Maybe even bring him to his knees ways of thanking him. Yes, I was definitely going to thoroughly thank Holland for taking such good care of my sister.

The rest of the day, we spent sitting around watching television and talking. Crimson opened up about her time with the sick fuck-faces that prostituted her out for their own profit. She told me how they auctioned off her virginity to the highest fucking bidder. Some old fat fuck who had a hard time even getting it up and blamed her. The fucker was lucky Crimson didn't know who he was because he'd be a dead fat fuck.

We ordered pizza about thirty minutes before Holland was due home. Crimson told me she usually made dinner for the two of them before she left for work and Holland made breakfast. I had to admit I was slightly jealous of their very domestic relationship. If it wasn't for the fact that they weren't fucking it would almost sound like they were in an actual relationship.

"Did you know that the woman who took me was Holland's mother?" We'd been watching a romantic comedy while we waited for the pizza when she blurted out that information.

"What the actual fuck? Please tell me you're kidding?" My first reaction is anger at Holland, even though I know from my own experience that sometimes your parents are complete assholes.

"Nope, it was her. She didn't even recognize him when he showed up either. This bitch tried to sell me to him to get her ass out of trouble." My mind is racing a mile a minute trying to piece everything together.

"Did he arrest her? Is she in jail for what she did?" My breath is coming out in short pants as my temper starts to rise.

"Nope bitch ran away right after trying to sell me. Holland's been trying to find her, but he hasn't had any luck. That bitch is slithery like a damn snake; she's probably hiding in some cave somewhere waiting to strike her next victim." He'd let her go, of course he did it was his own mother. I bet he wasn't looking very damn hard to find the skank whore bitch either. The woman who was responsible for my sister being used by men and he couldn't bring himself to arrest her because she was mommy fucking dearest. I was about to tell her to grab her shit we were leaving when Holland walked through the door.

"You sonofabitch!" I yelled at him.

"Woah, what the hell did I do? I've been at work all day. Is this one of those things where you watch something on TV and suddenly, I'm the bad guy kind of things?" He had the nerve to grin at me, didn't he know who he was messing with. I wasn't some young girl who would take his fucking excuses.

"Bella what the fuck? Why are you yelling at him?" Crimson stood up and got between the two of us.

"You're honestly going to stand there and defend his ass. He let his fucking mother get away with that shit. Don't you get it? He kept you here so you couldn't say anything to the cops. So his mother could get away with that shit." Crimson looked pissed and Holland looked like I'd slapped him in the face.

"Bella, you are way off base here. You don't know what you're talking about. He was going to let child services take me. I begged him not to, me not him." Holland put an arm on her shoulder.

"It's okay Crim, she doesn't know me. I get it. She doesn't know that I haven't seen my mother since she abandoned me and my sisters when we were little. That's why she didn't recognize me, because she doesn't know what the fuck her own son looks like!" Holland's chest was heaving, and his face was red with anger. But I didn't back down, not until Crimson broke down.

"It's not okay! Bella, if Holland hadn't found me you know where I would have wound up. You know. They would have taken me back there; you get that right. They would have found Mom and Dad and taken me back there. What part of, he fucking saved me, do you not get?" Crimson took off down the hall towards the small bedroom she used. Shame rolled over me, she was right if Holland hadn't taken her in child services would have taken her back to the same people who sold her.

"I'll go, tell Crimson I'll be back for her in the morning." I started to make my way to the door with my head down.

"Really that's it, you're just going to cuss me out and then walk away. I thought you had more gumption than that." Stopping with my hand on the knob, I turned to look at him.

He had this grin that made my panties practically melt right off of me. Why did he have to be so fucking hot? Every other cop I knew, not that I knew many, were fat, balding, middle aged ugly dudes.

"I just figured you'd want me out after I just chewed your ass for apparently nothing." Deep down I knew I owed him an apology, but I couldn't bring myself to say the words.

"I'm not going to kick you out simply because you yelled at me, Bella. Hell, if I kicked women out of my house every time they yelled at me I'd have fewer women staying at my house all the time." A sudden flare of jealousy took over me wondering what other fucking women he had staying at his house. None of my business that's who.

"Look I'm not going to force you to stay, but once Crimson calms down she'll see you were only pissed for her. She'll be hurt if you leave without her, she'll think...she'll think you left her." Before I can respond there's a knock on the door and when I pull it open the pizza delivery guy is there with a stack of boxes.

"Hello, I have a delivery for Crimson Nash." I heard Holland cuss under his breath before pulling out a couple of twenties for the kid as I took the boxes and made my way over to the kitchen table. Holland grabbed paper plates and napkins out of a cabinet in the kitchen. Somehow it felt like the most natural thing for us to be doing together, having dinner. Shit, this man could become an addiction very easily, good thing I was leaving tomorrow, which brought me back to my plans to thank him later.

Chapter Four

HOLLAND

Nothing like coming home to being yelled at by a woman. Not just any woman either, a fucking hot as hell, fire in her eyes women. She looked like she was ready to flay me alive for my imagined transgressions. When she realized how wrong she was she didn't even apologize, just tried to leave out the door like it never happened. No way was I letting that shit fly. Then add to that Crimson using my last name to order the pizza like we were married. I was surrounded by women who were trying to kill me one way or another.

"Oh Mrs. Nash, food's here." Bella's eyes got round as saucers, but she didn't say anything, instead it looked like she was trying to contain laughter. This wasn't something new that Crimson had pulled, no every chance Crimson got she'd insinuate that we were together as a couple. Some days I wanted to pull my hair out.

"Oh Mr. Nash, don't be such a prude, it's not like the pizza guy knows who Crimson is. For all he knew it was Bella. Chill dude." Crimson flounced into the dining area already in her work uniform. She didn't have a lot of time before she had to be there, but I wanted to make sure she ate.

"Not the point Crim, we talked about this." Bella watched our interaction with a smirk on her face.

"Are you finished being a bitch to my friend?" Crimson plopped down on the chair next to Bella giving her the stink eye.

"Crimson give your sister a break, she only wants to protect you. Her intentions are good, but she just doesn't understand all the facts. You can't blame her for thinking the way she did. Come on she came all this way to get you back, think about what that means." Crimson didn't say anything for a few minutes, and we ate in silence while she chewed over what I said. Since starting therapy, she's thought things through more before going off half-cocked on people.

"Fine, I'll forgive her, but she better be nice to you while I'm at work." Bella gave a little smirk at her sister.

"Don't worry I won't kill him while you're gone. Deal?" Bella wiped her hand off and reached across the table to Crimson.

"Deal!" Crimson pumped Bella's hand once and grinned.

"Good, now that you've gotten that squared away hurry up and eat. You gotta be at work shortly. Is Melanie bringing you home or do you want me to come pick you up?" Melanie was her boss and usually brought her home after the bar closed around two in the morning. I wasn't sure since she planned on quitting that night if she'd want to ride home with her soon to be ex-boss.

"I'll play it by ear, Mel might not want to give me a ride after I tell her I can't work there anymore." Crimson seemed a little sad at that thought. I knew she liked her job, but she wanted to go with her sister more.

"Sounds good, just call before eleven so I don't go to bed. You know how hard it is to wake me once I'm out." She nodded as she gulped down another slice of pizza. I didn't want her stranded trying to get home, not that this was her home anymore. That thought made me a little sad myself, we'd become our own little family. I wondered how much convincing it would take to get Bella to just stay, but I knew that was a lost cause. She didn't even like me.

"Do you want to ride with us when I drop her off?" I asked Bella.

"Afraid I might rob you blind again?" She asked with a smile.

"Yup, you caught me I'm afraid you'll take off with my five-year-old television and my CDs of Johnny Cash." I smirked back at her.

"Shit, you didn't tell me anything about Johnny Cash CD's Crim! You were holding out on me." Crimson shook her head.

"Har, har, har Bell. Come on I want to show you where I've been working. It's a nice place, no strippers or drugs." It was comments like that one that made me cringe for her sometimes. She didn't have a lot of good things in her life, and it showed.

"Damn no strippers or drugs what kind of bar is this. Sounds fancy." Bella followed us out and scooted into the middle of the bench seat of my old truck until she was flush against my side.

"Oh, this is nice a truck, I bet it's seen a lot of action, especially this bench seat." I knew what she was getting at, but I focused on the road instead of the raging hard on I had from images she provoked.

"Oh yeah I love Holl's truck, but he still won't let me drive it. Says it's his baby, but he offered to help me buy a car eventually. Guess I won't be needing that help after all Holl, might call you for advice though. If that's alright?" Crimson again sounded disappointed and a little sad. It made me want to tell her she didn't have to leave, that she could stay if she wanted to.

"Of course, you can Crim. You know I'm still here for you if you need something. A friend, help, anything I'm here." I need her to know that I'm not abandoning her, even though she's the one leaving.

"Yeah, I know, I don't know why I'm being so needy. I know, I know before you say it. It's not needy to express your needs to those around you. It's called communicating." She changed her voice, so it was deeper to imitate my voice. Bella and I both chuckled.

"Exactly, now have a good night and call me if you need me to pick you up." We'd arrived at the bar and Crimson hopped out of the truck quickly. I figured Bella would scoot over once Crimson was out of the truck; instead, she seemed very content to stay where she was. We both waved to Crimson when she turned around at the front door and watched her walk inside.

"You've done a good job. In case you didn't know." Bella murmured as I pulled out of the parking lot. It meant a lot to me to hear her say that.

"Thank you. I just want her to have a chance. That's what anyone who's been through what she has deserves." Bella reached out and grabbed my hand giving it a squeeze.

"You're right she deserves that chance to be happy. You've helped give that to her." I'd just pulled into my drive when she reached up and turned my head toward her. I thought she wanted to look me in eye, but instead she leaned up and kissed me. As soon as our lips met my entire body came to life.

My hands found her their way into her hair and gripped her tightly as I deepened the kiss. Suddenly she shifted and was in my lap moaning and rubbing her core against my cock that was straining against my jeans. I'd probably have a fucking indention on it from my zipper at the rate we were going. Pulling back, I looked into her eyes.

"This is a bad idea. Tell me this is a bad idea." Instead of telling me it was a bad idea, she yanked me to her lips once more. Her hands pulled my shirt up 'til she could get underneath to skim my chest with her nails.

"House. Need a bed. Want to make you scream." I said between kisses as I opened the truck door, and we made our way into the house.

"Just for tonight." She whispered against my lips. I wanted more, but right at that moment; I'd take whatever she was willing to give so I nodded.

As soon as the door was shut, clothes started coming off. I heard buttons hit the floor when she yanked my shirt open and flung it somewhere across the room. This woman was like fire and if I wasn't careful, she'd brand me for life as hers. I could easily see myself falling for her and not just because of her hot fucking body. There was something about her that called to me.

When she was down to her bra and panties, I brought her flush against my body so I could touch every single inch of her curves. If I was only going to have her for one night, I was going to make sure it was a memorable one for both of us. Gripping her ass, I lifted her up wrapping her legs around my waist and carried her back to my room without breaking contact with our lips.

Laying her out on the bed, she was all lush curves and sin staring back up at me.

"You going to just take in the sights or play with them." She ran her hands from her hips up to her breasts before stretching out like a satisfied cat. Fuck she was beautiful.

"Oh, I'm going to play with them; I just like to admire beautiful things when I see them." A light blush spread from her head to her toes. Reaching for the waistband of her panties I slowly pulled them down her legs, bending a little to kiss a trail down to the top of her mound. She smelled fucking delectable, so I dipped my tongue just a little to tease her and she moaned out my name.

Gripping her thighs, I pulled her to the edge of the bed and got down on my knees. Fuck moaning out my name, I was going to make her chat it like a prayer. Running my tongue along her slit, I let it slide in until I hit her clit.

"Holy shit!" Nope not the words I want her to be yelling yet. Gotta try harder. Latching onto her clit, I nibbled it until she was arching into me. Then I slid two fingers inside her wetness and started pumping slowly until she was grinding against my hand.

"Holland please...please." Her head was thrashing from side to side while her fingers had a death grip on my hair. I was pretty sure I'd have half-moon indents in my scalp from her nails, and I gave zero fucks.

"Something else you wanting sweetness?" I asked as I reached in my nightstand for a condom.

"Yes, now give it to me before I take it." There was that fire I was falling for. Sliding the condom on myself I rubbed my cock against her wet opening. I could feel the warmth emanating from her, welcoming me. She growled in frustration at my teasing, so I dipped just the tip in. Bella moaned out in pleasure.

"Is this what you are wanting?" I slid about half the way in, and she grabbed for my hips pulling me all the way in.

"Ah hell!" I hissed out she felt so fucking good wrapped around my cock. Like the perfect fucking glove. Bella reached around behind her back releasing her bra before flinging it across the room. God her breasts were beautiful and were begging for my mouth to be on them. Latching onto her nipple, I sucked hard which brought a hum of approval.

"Fuck Bella, what are you doing to me." I always made fun of guys who got pussy whipped but right about now I could totally understand why they did. Being inside her made me forget everything else around me.

"Don't stop, don't you dare fucking stop." She begged as I grabbed her hips and started pumping harder. Rubbing my thumb against her clit, I could see her release coming. It was only a matter of minutes, maybe even seconds, before she was going to detonate, and I wasn't going to be far behind her. Her whole body convulsed as she reached the peak of her orgasm. Her nails raked down my back, her legs became vice grips, and her pussy pulsated around me.

"Fuck. Holland. Holland. Holland." She chanted as I pounded into her again and again chasing my own release.

"Holy shiiit!" I yelled as I curled my body around her, drawing out both of our orgasms as long as possible. There's a moment where I'm pretty sure she snatched my soul out of my body as I rolled off of her. Hurrying into the bathroom, I disposed of the condom and crawled back into bed pulling her against me. She stiffened for a moment before relaxing against me.

I woke the next morning knowing immediately that she was gone. The warmth of her body was gone; the only thing that lingered was her soft vanilla scent. Figuring she got up so she could get ready to leave I jumped out of bed. Silence greeted me as I made my way through the house. Crimson's bag was gone, and when I looked outside so was Bella's bike. There was a note taped to the frig, it wasn't in Crimson's handwriting, so I assumed it was Bella who wrote it.

Holland,

I'm glad I got a chance to thank you properly last night for everything you've done for Crimson. She wanted to say goodbye, but I didn't want to wake you. Thank you again for being there for her when I couldn't.

Bella & Crimson

Something in my chest felt heavy at that moment, like all the air had been sucked out of the room. I felt disgusted with myself thinking that she only gave herself to me as a thank you for helping her sister. She'd always view me as all the other men in her life because of that. Fuck! I stood there looking at my door hoping they would come back. But life doesn't work that way for me, never has and never will. People leave me, that's just the way it is.

Chapter Five

The Present

HOLLAND

They say when life gives you lemons make lemonade. What about when life hands you a shit sandwich with a side of fucked up fries? What do you do then? How about when your own mother is your downfall, the one who finally breaks you, what do you do then? First it was Bliss, then it was dealing with Crimson, then Beth, and now dealing with the fallout from my sisters' kidnapping. When the fuck was, I going to get a break? Apparently not today, as I stepped into the precinct to the sounds of my Sergeant, Bellamy, yelling my name.

"He sounds pissed, man." Ramirez, one of the patrol guys, hissed under his breath. When I glared over at him, he turtled up and skidded around me.

"NASH! Nash, get your ass in here now!" Oh goodie, this fuckwit wanted to ream my ass, let the yelling match begin.

Stepping into the Sergeant's office, I notice he's sitting behind his desk tapping his fingers with impatience. Sergeant Bellamy only had a few more years before he retired, and it showed. His potbelly hung over his slacks, barely contained in his button up shirt. He started balding a few years prior and was now at the comb-over stage, the only problem was he only had a few hairs to comb-over.

"Yeah Sarge, you wanted to see me?" I asked as casually as possible sitting down in one of the chairs across from his desk. I'd taken a risk getting Bart's crew to help me find my sisters, a risk that paid off thankfully. Now I was pretty sure I wasn't about to get rewarded for my risk.

"What the fuck were you thinking going to the Hades Rejects for help?" My eyes narrowed on him, but before I could answer he put his hand up to stop me.

"I know your sisters were in danger, but that doesn't mean you go rogue. We have procedures for a damn reason." I wanted to tell him yeah procedures that would have allowed my sisters to remain in the sick situation they were in, but I kept my mouth shut. Once I started, I wasn't sure I'd be able to keep from dragging him across the desk and beating the shit out of him.

"I'm going to find evidence you were there and then I'm going to nail your ass. You can't just go vigilante like that whenever it benefits you." I fisted the chair's arms struggling to control myself. This piece of shit had no idea what my sisters went through, they wouldn't even tell me everything that happened to them.

"You're on suspension while they investigate your involvement in the murder of everyone in that warehouse." Damn right all those fuckers were dead, Bart and the Rejects helped me make sure of that.

"Anything else Sarge?" I gritted out between my teeth, barely containing myself. He sighed like he was defeated suddenly, like he was trying to look like he gave a shit.

"Look Nash, you should have known that eventually this would happen. You can't be friends with the likes of those guys and not expect to be pulled into their shit. Get yourself clear of them; it could save your career." The likes of those guys, the ones who risked their lives to rescue my sisters. I needed to get myself clear of them.

"My father is one of those guys, my best friends are those guys, and they're better men than you'll ever be." I leaned over the desk right into his face, my eyes full of the fury I felt down to my fucking toes.

"Here, this doesn't mean what I thought it did." I handed over my badge and gun.

"I thought we went after the real bad guys. We don't, we go after the guys who look guilty simply because they wear leather jackets and ride motorcycles. That's bullshit and you know it." I walked to the open door, where everyone in the section could hear me.

"I thought I was joining a brotherhood, but y'all wouldn't know true brotherhood if it slapped you in the face." I didn't bother to look back as I walked out of the job, I'd dreamed of having since I was kid.

Getting in my truck, I slammed my hands against the steering wheel in frustration. I would never regret what I did to get my sisters back, but it hurt to know that it cost me my dream. The truth was things had felt off since Bliss's situation. I'd known then that I was steering into the grey area more and more. How much longer until I was completely in the black? 'Til I became a dirty cop trying to justify everything I did as long as I got the bad guy?

So where did I go from here, what was my next step? I had no fucking clue, but I knew who could help me figure it out. The men who knew what true brotherhood meant, who stood by me when I needed them the most. Men who bled for me, who would bleed for me again if I needed them to, that's who. Sometimes when you try to avoid the inevitable it catches up to you and drags you in. I'd avoided the inevitable for a long time, but I couldn't anymore. I belong with them; they were my brotherhood, my family, my solid place to land when shit got deep.

Pulling out of the station parking lot was like the final nail in the coffin of my career with the police department. Maybe I failed them; maybe they failed me, who knew for sure which it was. One thing was certain, it wasn't where I needed to be anymore. As I drove, it was like a weight was lifted off my shoulders. I didn't feel like I had to fit the mold that I forced myself to fit anymore. My father told me when I joined the police academy that the club would be there waiting when I was ready. I remember laughing at him, determined that my future was the police force. Instead of being pissed he hugged me, told me he loved me, and he understood I needed to find my way on my own.

Damn it, now I'd have to tell him he was right! I laughed out loud in the cab of my truck knowing he was going to enjoy saying he told me so. The closer I got to the clubhouse the more my nerves started taking over. What if I was making a mistake? No, without them I wouldn't have my sisters back. It was that simple, they had my back when the men who were supposed to didn't.

Rolling to a stop inside the compound several of the club members, who were outside chilling, glanced my way. My anxiety was kicking up just thinking about talking to Pops. I've known Pops practically my whole life, hell he was basically a second father to me and my sisters, but I was still nervous. He could laugh at me and tell me to get the hell out of his club, or he could open his arms and welcome me in. It was tough to say, but the only way I was getting an answer was to go inside and ask the question.

"Yo, Holly!" Matt yelled from his seat at a wooden picnic table waving his hand like a maniac smiling as I got out of my truck.

"You ain't here to arrest us are you man?" I narrowed my eyes at him.

"First of all, dude, stop calling me Holly. The twins are bad enough calling me that shit. Second, no I'm not here to arrest you. Why you done something you need arresting for? Wait, don't answer that question, of course you have." We both had secrets, but until I was patched in some of those secrets needed to remain secrets. Matt jumped up from the picnic table, kissing his girl Jesse on the cheek before intercepting me from going inside the club.

"Awe, come on Holly, don't be like that. Come give me a hug man." Before I could dodge out of his way, he had me in a bear hug. I swear he was trying to crush my ribs, or maybe just crack my back. Then I felt his hands shuffling around my body and I realized he was actually fucking frisking me.

"What the fuck man? When have I ever needed to be fucking frisked to get into the club before?" Alarm bells started going off in my head. If he was being cautious even with me something was going on.

"What's going on? Is Bliss safe? What about Pops? My dad? For fuck's sake Matt stop fucking grinning and tell me why the fuck you're frisking me." Matt just shook his head jutting his chin toward the clubhouse door.

"Go talk to Pops, he'll fill you in on what you need to know. I'm just following orders, they don't include you exactly, but I was told anyone wanting inside had to be checked. Sorry man, you know better than anyone, orders are orders." He hadn't answered a damn one of my fucking questions, fucking asshole.

"You should really think about cutting back on that cussing there though Holly, it's very unprofessional. Aren't they on your asses about being professional?" Matt smirked before walking back to the picnic table he was sitting on with his girl. Taking a deep breath, I focused on the task at hand and not wanting to beat Matt's ass.

"Yeah, well I don't have to worry about being professional anymore. But you'll find out soon all about that, I need to talk to Pops first." That got Matt's attention as his eyes got as big as saucers in surprise. Everyone else at the table glanced back and forth between the two of us, trying to decipher what I'd meant. Matt knew, he'd figured it out quickly, and by the look on Jesse's face she'd figured it out too.

"Shit man, I'm sorry. I know how much that shit meant to you." Matt was an asshole, but he was still one of my best friends. He knew how much I'd struggled with my decision to become a cop and was there when I finally got the courage up to tell my dad.

"Yeah, well shit changes man, you know that as well as I do." I jerked my chin to his girl sitting beside him. It wasn't too long ago that his girl, Jesse, was struggling with some heavy shit, but he'd helped her work through her issues. Things hadn't been easy, but then again nothing worth having was.

"Yeah man, I know shit changes." Matt looked over at his girl like she hung the fucking moon and she looked at him like he was the center of her damn universe. This was a different Matt from a few years ago, this was a man in love, and I couldn't be happier for him, but damn it I wanted that shit.

"Sometimes the changes make life worth living though man, just remember that." I nodded in understanding as I made my way inside the clubhouse.

The clubhouse hadn't changed much since I was a kid running around, fetching drinks for my dad or one of the other club members. Things back then were simpler; I was completely oblivious to all the illegal shit the club was doing. I could just enjoy the camaraderie, the sense of brotherhood that seemed to permeate the air, and it always felt like one big family. When the blinders came off about the illegal activities the club was into, I couldn't stick around. Something inside me demanded truth, justice, and order.

There was a time I thought about joining the military, but I knew that wasn't where I could do the most good for my community. The police force called to me, they claimed that they were a family, a brotherhood, and I thought it was the perfect solution. Turns out, I was wrong, seriously wrong.

"Well smack my ass and call me Sally, look what the cat dragged in guys." Bart yelled from the bar, tipping his beer towards me.

"Come have a drink with me man, I haven't seen you since we got the twins back." It looked like Bart was well on his way to being drunk, and it was only five in the evening.

"How are they doing? Your dad doesn't say much, but I can tell it's been rough on him. Matt's brothers keep trying to talk to them, but they have been holed up with your dad refusing to see them." Bart was talking loud enough for the whole club to hear my sister's business and I didn't like it. Haley and Harley had already been through enough without having to deal with gossip.

"They're fine, they need time to heal." I spoke quietly to him, hoping he'd get the point.

"You should know how that is, Bliss needed time to heal, remember." Bart looked a little green when I mentioned Bliss. They were expecting their first baby soon, but before they got together, Bliss had been brutally raped by her ex-boyfriend. We didn't find her in time, yet another reason I should have already left the force, because I couldn't get the information, I needed to track him down soon enough.

"Yeah, I get it man. I need to call my girl." I nodded as he pulled out his cell phone to call her.

"Baby, can you come pick me up?" He paused while listening to whatever Bliss said.

"Yeah, I was celebrating with the guys." He put his hand over the receiver looking at me.

"We're having a girl." He smiled as he went back to talking to his girl and I walked towards Pop's office.

Chapter Six

BELLA

"I'm not leaving you!" Crimson looked close to tears.

"You can't face them alone, I'm staying." I loved my little sister's stubbornness, but in times like these, I hated it. I needed her to run as far and as fast as she could away from this place.

"I'm not going to face them alone; I have the club backing me." Crimson gave me a look that said she wasn't buying what I was selling.

"Okay I have most of the club backing. Fine they're all throwing me to the fucking wolves happy!" You piss off the wrong guy and suddenly your entire club, that you're president of, is tossing you out. Admittedly, the guy I pissed off was Lorenzo Bianchi, one of Chicago's notorious gangsters, but we were supposed to have each other's backs.

Figures they would abandon me as soon as shit got too deep though.

You go to one nightclub, get hit on by one fine mofo, you start dancing with the fine ass man only to find out he's Lorenzo Bianchi. Now normally I don't mind gangsters, I love a hot bad boy, they do it for me. But Lorenzo's outfit was linked to the sex slave trade and after what happened to Crimson there was no way I was getting involved with that shit.

Lorenzo didn't take my rebuff very well; alright he was downright pissed. He tried to forcibly remove me from the club; I could still feel the bruises he left on my upper arm. Thankfully we were in public and we weren't in Chicago. I fought like a wild woman scratching and kicking until the bouncers at the club stepped in. While he was distracted by the bouncers, I got the fuck out of there as quickly as possible.

I didn't think he would find me; I didn't think he'd be able to track me down, I was wrong. The next day not only did he find me, but he sent me a very clear message in the form of my VP Mongo's body. They dumped him right on the front steps on the clubhouse with a note demanding I return to him. At first the club was pissed, they wanted revenge, until they found out who it was. They wanted nothing to do with Lorenzo and his gang; honestly, I couldn't really blame them. I didn't want anything to do with him and his gang either.

Instead of waiting for them to turn on me completely I grabbed Crimson and we hauled ass to Kentucky. My husband, Cain "Cash" Graves, the previous president of the Riddler's Ryders MC left me with lots of places we could hide. At least he was good for something, he wasn't good for much when he was alive, but at least he'd given me a place to run to. Marrying him had to have been the biggest mistake of my life, one I never planned to repeat, ever again. He got me out of my parent's house, which was exactly what I needed at the time.

When we met, he was the perfect bad boy I needed, willing to do whatever it took to keep me by his side, sound familiar. It wasn't until three months into our blissful married life that the real Cain came out. The first time he hit me I was so in shock I didn't even react at first. I kept thinking that there was no way he would ever touch me like that. He apologized of course, begged forgiveness, and said it was the stress of dealing with the club business. Stupid me, I forgave him again and again.

The day he started using club whores for his needs, I remember breathing a sigh of relief thinking that meant he wouldn't want to touch me anymore. I was wrong, and the more I fought him, the worse it was for me. He wanted a son, a boy to carry on his name, to become his sucessor. What he didn't know was that I was on birth control, and there was no way I was ever giving him a kid to raise. By that time, I was resigned to the fact that one day he'd kill me, and then a miracle happened.

All right so it wasn't really a miracle, more like an act of Karma, but still it benefited me. Cain and most of the club were on a ride together, when a semi-truck plowed into the whole group. The club was left with nothing but old ladies, their kids, and a few prospects. After all the funerals, everyone started looking to me for guidance, someone to lead them, and my dumbass agreed to step in as president at least temporarily.

Soon temporary turned into a permanent position once I started running things. I promoted the prospects to full patch members, recruited some guys with skills that would be assets to the club, and figured out ways to make profits rise. I bought a few titty bars and an auto body shop. The old ladies ran the titty bars, and the guys ran the body shop, we were doing good, until I pissed off the wrong man. Our club couldn't sustain a hit like something Lorenzo could throw at us. I knew they were making a hard choice, but I still held out hope that they would stick by me. Unfortunately, their desire to survive outweighed their loyalty to me.

"You can't face him alone Bella and I'm not letting you. We're in this together, remember, you promised we'd never separate again." Crimson's chin wobbled a little and her eyes shined with unshed tears. Fuck, what had I gotten us into?

"I know honey, and if there was any other way to keep you safe, I'd do it. But eventually they will find us. Lorenzo is a man with many connections; I can't let them get ahold of you. Not after…" Damn it just thinking about what my sister went through makes my throat threaten to close up on me.

"Not after what you went through, I won't put you at risk of that ever happening again." No fucking way in hell I was letting Lorenzo's goons get ahold of my sister just to put her right back into the same situation when Holland found her. I should have left her at Holland's, I should have never gone after her, she'd be safely tucked away with him if I hadn't been so selfish. But what was done was done, now I needed to convince her to run.

"Where the hell am, I supposed to go? Huh?" She folded her arms over her chest giving me an attitude.

"Back home? So, they can sell me again? Bella, I have nowhere to go and you know that." But she did have somewhere she could go; she just didn't want to say it. She tried to get me to go back and really talk to Holland, but I refused. Somehow, she knew there was something between us, some kind of magnetic pull, but I wasn't about to go down that road again. I fell for one man; no way was I falling for another. But he was the safest place for her, he had connections with the Hades Rejects, he was a cop, and he'd protect her.

"You know where you gotta go." Crimson shook her head at me smirking.

"Don't start, this is for your safety, nothing else. Once I think it's safe, I'll come get you again, and we'll ride off into the sunset together. Two sisters ready to raise hell." I pulled her in for a hug, holding her for as long as she would let me before she started complaining I was crushing her.

"Sure, I'll go right back to Holland and tell him what exactly. Oh, do you mind me crashing here while my sister is off getting raped or murdered for turning some douchebag down. How does that sound?" I loved my sister, but lord help me if she didn't work my nerves to the point of no return some days.

"Are you fucking crazy? No, that's not what you say. You tell him as little as possible; you should know this. Just tell him you need a place to stay while I get some things straightened out for us. He does not need to know anything else about our lives, capeesh?" I didn't need or want his help out of this situation. He was a good guy; he didn't need to be involved with the dirty shit I was dealing with. Good guys like him deserved women who weren't damaged goods.

"You're thinking about him, aren't you? Why can't you just admit you have the hots for him? I mean the man is fine. And he's a decent guy too, he never took me up on my offers. Bella, you deserve that kind of guy in your corner." She was wrong; I didn't deserve a guy that good in my life. Maybe in my previous life, when I daydreamed about being married and having kids, living happily ever after, but my parents ruined that dream.

When I found out they planned to sell me I had two options: either let them do it or run. I ran, right into the arms of Cain, right into the fires of Hell. I'm not so sure it was the lesser of two evils, but I couldn't go back in time. Cain served his purpose, I was free, I'd earned my freedom, and I'd die before I became another man's property.

"Crimson, just do as I say. Please. I need you safe somewhere while I deal with this shit." I needed her somewhere safe; Holland was safe. According to Crimson, he practically walked on water. Who could blame her though? The man took her in, gave her a safe place to stay, and asked nothing in return other than she went to therapy and got a job. He didn't even take any of her money from her job, he let her spend the money on whatever she wanted.

"Fine, but I can't promise you I'll keep my mouth shut about what you've gotten yourself into. He's going to figure out I'm not just visiting real quick. Bella he's not stupid, the guy's a cop, he solves crime for a fucking living. He'll be able to see right through any lies I tell him. Please just come with me and we can hide out at his place 'til this blows over." Crimson's eyes pleaded with me, and there was a part of me that really wanted to give in. I needed to handle this myself, I didn't need a white knight to come in and slay my dragons. I hugged her tight one last time before we got her ready to head out, hoping it wasn't the last time I'd see her.

Chapter Seven

HOLLAND

"You guys are assholes, the whole lot of you." I groaned as I continued to clean the grease off the garage floor. Being a fucking prospect sucked donkey dick, what made it worse was when my buddies stood around watching me for their own amusement, dicks.

"Now Holly, is that anyway to talk to your betters? Tisk Tisk." Matt bent over laughing, grabbing Bart to hold himself up. It was bad enough they got to rib my ass every damn day, but Matt took it upon himself to give me an unofficial road name of Holly. I couldn't wait to get patched in so I could tear him a new asshole.

"Leave him alone Matt, don't you remember when you were prospecting. They had you on toilet detail every weekend for like two months straight." Bart smirked as Matt turned a little green around the gills. I shuddered thinking about having to clean toilets for the club for two months during weekend parties. Fuck that! I'd take grease clean up any day over that shit.

"That wasn't cool man, I think I might lose my lunch. Fucking asshole!" Matt punched Bart in the arm before making a beeline to the garbage can in the corner of the garage.

"That was just mean, babe." Bliss sauntered up to Bart, running her fingers up his chest, pressing her breasts against him.

"Jesse won't be happy he's throwing up the lunch she made him." I chuckled to myself, thinking about how Jesse might make Bart pay for making her man sick to his stomach.

"I didn't know he'd throw up. Not my fault he has a weak constitution. Quit being a big baby!" Bart hollered over at Matt who was still leaned over the garbage can hurling.

"Damn it! Once he starts, he can't stop. You better go get Jesse so she can take him home." I almost felt bad for my friend, until I remembered he was just giving me shit not five seconds earlier.

"Hey, isn't that your girlfriend Holland?" Bliss asked and my head snapped up, my first thought was one of my exes found out I was prospecting for the Hades Rejects and wanted another go. Instead, I saw Crimson, looking exhausted walking towards us.

"Not my fucking girlfriend, she's just a damn kid. Jesus you know me better than that woman." I hadn't heard from her since she'd left, even though she swore she'd keep in contact. Once she was back with her sister though I figured I wouldn't ever see her again. By the looks of her something was wrong, and my protective instincts were kicking in. Standing up I dusted off my hands on the front of my worn jeans I'd been wearing to clean the grease up and waited for her to get closer.

"She looks older. How the fuck am I supposed to know? You never explained to any of us why she was living with you or who the fuck she was. I'm going to go get Jesse." Bart gave me a dirty look as his woman walked away in a huff.

"She has a point man. You weren't exactly forth coming in the details where she was concerned." He was right, but things back then were fucked up. Not that they were much better now, but when I took Crimson in, I wasn't in a good place with the club.

"After everything we've all been through a little info probably would have been a good idea." He was right, if I wanted to be a part of the club, I needed to tell them everything.

"I'll explain as soon as I find out why she's here, I swear." Crimson stopped in front of me, squinting as she took in my new vest.

"What the fuck Holland you're a fucking Reject now? Shit! That's not going to work, that's not going to work at all. You were a fucking cop; you were supposed to be a fucking good guy." I couldn't help but smile, because no matter how many times I tried to get her to curb her cursing it never worked. She looked crushed to find out I was trying to be a Reject though, like it somehow ruined her life. Which didn't really make sense, I looked behind her for her sister, but I didn't see her or her badass bike. Something wasn't right.

"Crimson, why are you here?" She looked down at her shoes, kicking a stray pebble.

"Crimson, where is your sister?" When she looked back up at me, there were tears in her eyes.

"She made me go, said she couldn't take care of things and worry about me. I didn't want to go, but she made me." The tears started running down her face and I pulled her into a hug.

"They're going to kill her, or worse. You gotta help her. But you can't now." What the hell was she talking about? If Bella was in trouble me being a cop or not shouldn't matter.

"Who? Who is going to kill her? Crimson you have to give me something to go on here kid. If your sister is in trouble I can help." She shook her head against my chest, giant sobs echoing in the garage. Bart looked just as perplexed, while Matt finally joined the party still looking a little green.

"You can't help anymore. You were supposed to still be a cop. But now you're this, and she won't want this." Crimson backed away, flinging her hand out to point to my cut like it was a spider she wanted to squash.

"What's she talking about? Dude you have the worst taste in women." I glared at Matt, thinking of all the ways I was going to beat the shit out of him once I was no longer a prospect. Before I could correct him though, Jesse came barreling into the garage looking concerned for Matt.

"Matt, babe. Are you alright? You look awful, let's get you home." Jesse put her arm around Matt trying to steer him towards the door.

"Oh, hi Crimson." Matt looked at his girl like she'd grown two heads.

"You know this chick babe? How do you know her but we don't?" Jesse blushed as she looked over at me to explain, which made Matt growled.

"Because she helped me get her a job, dumbass. Crimson, meet Matt and Bart, my asshole friends and future brothers." Not that I didn't think of them as my brothers already, but once I was patched, they'd be my club brothers. Crimson clung to me as she waved to the idiots.

"And again, not my girlfriend. She was never my girlfriend." Matt just rolled his eyes like he didn't believe a word I said.

"She's fucking seventeen, I'm not a goddamn pedophile asshole." Matt's eyes looked like they were about to fall out of their sockets.

"Then who the fuck is she numnuts? Because we definitely don't need no fucking jailbait running around the club." I ran my hand down my face, sighing to myself.

"You don't listen to a damn thing I say do you? I told you about her like forever ago dude. She's the girl my mom and Jack had working." Crimson looked down at her shoes in embarrassment. The kid didn't have shit to be embarrassed about as far as I was concerned, but clearly, she didn't like people knowing about her past.

"She stayed with me for a little bit, while I searched for her sister. Only her sister found me instead." I figured keeping shit simple was probably the way to go. Crimson story was Crimson's to tell, not mine.

"Yeah, only then she got herself in to some deep shit with some asshole because she turned him down and now you can't help because you're a fucking prospect. I needed a fucking cop, not this." She threw her hand up in exasperation at me as she turned to walk away. What the fuck was she rambling on about?

"Crimson wait, where's Bella? Tell me what the fuck is going on." I reached out and grabbed her elbow, stopping her escape. Before I knew what was happening, she planted the heel of her boot down my shin to my foot, then elbowed me hard in the stomach, making me double over in pain.

"What the fuck Crimson?" I gasped out, holding my stomach.

"Oh shit, I'm sorry Holland, it was a knee-jerk reaction. See I remember all the shit you taught me; no guy is going to be able to take advantage of me again." I was torn between pride that she remembered all my self-defense techniques and wanting to curl into a little ball from the pain.

"Damn girl that was badass! How come you haven't taught me, Jesse, and Beth those moves? Huh?" Bliss stood over me hands on her hips looking like an avenging angel ready to strike.

"You've never asked first of all and second of all, you and Beth know how to shoot and carry a fucking gun these days. Jesse until recently, thanks to Matt, has been terrified of her own shadow. No way was I going to practice that shit with her and scare her half to death." Bliss tapped her boot against the pavement like she was waiting for the rest of my answer.

"Do you want me to teach you self-defense Bliss?" I sighed out as Matt and Bart both coughed behind their hands to keep from laughing.

"Yes, I would, but not right now. Right now, it sounds like your girl needs help or someone she knows does. Honestly everything you said was very confusing." We all gave Crimson our full attention.

"Fine, I'll tell you, but it won't do any good, you're just a prospect." We listened intently as Crimson relayed everything from when Bella refused Lorenzo to them hiding out in the mountains. The more she talked the more anxious I became to get the fuck out of there and go find her. If Lorenzo found her there was no telling what he might do, but whatever it was, it wasn't going to be good. I needed to make sure I found her first, by any means necessary.

Chapter Eight

BELLA

"Little pig, little pig, let me in." Shit, shit, fucking shit. Time was up. I was out of places to hide and Lorenzo's men were seconds from finding me. At least Crimson wasn't here with me, I couldn't live with myself if they captured her too. After everything she'd already been through, she didn't deserve to get pulled into my mess. She was safe with Holland, damn just thinking about him made my heart rate pick up. No, that was the fear of the guys about to break down the door of the cabin I was hiding in that had my heart rate picking up.

Stifling a scream with the palm of my hand, I prayed, for the first time in my life, as the front door finally caved in. Maybe they wouldn't find the door under the rug. I hoped. The cellar was my last best hope at hiding from them. If I could stay quiet and they didn't look too closely at the floor I might live to fight another day. Light spilled through the spaces in the floor, I could make out several figures moving around the cabin.

"Come out, come out, wherever you are. And maybe we'll deliver you to the boss without trying out the goods." I scooted as far back into the cellar as I could away from Lorenzo's goons' voice.

"Shut the fuck up Marcel, she won't come out if she thinks we're going to touch her. Damn it, you've probably just lost us any chance at getting her to come out. We've been tracking this bitch for the last month, she's not stupid." I watched through the floor slat as two of Lorenzo's goons seemed to have it out. I'm guessing the one getting manhandled is Marcel. Maybe they would give up trying to find me if I could evade them a little longer.

"Come on Victor, she ain't coming out no matter what we say. And she can't be that smart, she turned down Lorenzo. What woman turns down a man like him? A stupid one I tell you." Victor shook his head before pushing Marcel back a little. Well now this was interesting; it looked like not all was roses in Lorenzo's camp of followers. Maybe he could be an ally if I'm captured, maybe he'd help me escape.

"And that right there is how we all know you don't know shit when it comes to women. Not all of them need or want a man in power. This chick obviously had power herself, before her little motorcycle club bailed on her, so she didn't want or need Lorenzo's." Well Victor clearly knew how women think, or at least some of what we think.

"I'm hoping now that they ditched her she'll be more apt to take him up on his offer. But honestly, I don't give a shit as long as I get to go home and get the fuck out of the damn boonies. Now help search." All right Victor was still a dickwad so much for maybe finding an ally in Lorenzo's crew.

They started moving about the cabin. I could hear doors being opened and shut swiftly; they must have been looking through the cabinets. A big bang, that had me muffling my screech again, sounded from the back bedroom area. They must have flipped the big ass bed in the room, hoping I was hiding under it. Dust started filtering down on me making it harder for me to see anything. The couch and loveseat took a dive next, as they flipped them over, not that I could hide under them, they just wanted to destroy shit.

"She's not fucking here!" Victor growled out as he stomped around the living room.

"Where the fuck could she have gone? Her fucking car is here, there's no way in or out except the way we came, and we've been watching that road for two days with nobody coming or going. She has to fucking be here!" Victor shouted the last bit right before I heard the crash of the small kitchen table hitting the floor.

"What if she went out into the woods? Like some kind of survivalist shit." Marcel suggested. I smiled to myself hoping they might latch onto that idea. If they thought I was out in the woods they might split up and try to find me out there.

"I seriously doubt she went all Rambo on us, but let's at least check the perimeter to see if we can find any tracks leading away from here. She might just be hiding somewhere close by waiting for us to leave. I'd say the only way she knows how to survive is by spreading her legs, but the bitch has been giving us the slip for the past month. FUCK!" Victor stomped out of the cabin followed by the rest of Lorenzo's goons. I let out a sigh of relief as I heard them yelling at each other from outside. They weren't very bright if they thought yelling for me was going to get me to come out of hiding.

It felt like hours passed before I heard their car start and the gravel kick up from their exit. I knew deep down they wouldn't go far; they knew I was here somewhere. Waiting an extra few minutes to be sure they didn't come right back, I inched my way out of my hiding spot. Luckily when they tossed the living room the love seat only landed slightly on the hidden door, but I still had to push pretty hard to get it to move.

"Fuck!" I grunted as I used my shoulder to push, it finally gave way, and I was able to climb out. Looking around the cabin it looked like a rampaging bull visited me. Everything was upended, my clothes were strewn all over the bedroom, and my table was utterly destroyed in the dining area. Lorenzo's men would need to regroup, probably call him to find out what he wanted them to do next. Hopefully, that would keep them busy long enough for me to grab some shit and make a run for it.

Snatching up my clothes that were thrown all over the floor, I quickly packed what I could in a small bag. I had to keep moving, if I could just keep moving, I could avoid capture. Somehow, I knew that I wasn't going to be able to avoid being captured forever, but I had to try. There was no way I was just going to give up without putting up some kind of fight. I made my way through the wreckage that was left of the front door only to be greeted by the sound of guns being cocked.

"Well. Well. Well, look what we have here gentlemen. Looks like our little rabbit came out of her hole." I glared at Marcel as I looked around to the five thugs aiming their weapons at me. Maybe I could make it back inside before they shot me, but where would I go?

"Don't even think about it little rabbit, you're surrounded. Now put the bag down and come with us nicely." Oh, this fucker didn't know who he was dealing with. Nicely wasn't even in my vocabulary, let alone something I knew how to do.

Throwing my bag at Marcel's face, I sprinted toward the woods, hoping I could clear the trees before they got a shot off. I knew Lorenzo wanted me alive; I was counting on him wanting me in one piece too.

"Sonofabitch! Get her! You cunt! I'm going to enjoy watching him break you." Marcel raged as the bullets began to fly.

"Marcel you fucking idiot! I gave you one fucking job, and you couldn't even fucking do that right. Don't fucking hit her!" Victor's voice rang out from somewhere behind the cabin. Marcel hadn't been lying, I was surrounded, but I was just a few feet from the trees. If I could make it into the trees, I could hide, but just as I reached the tree line, a hard body slammed into me bringing me down.

Twisting and clawing at my attacker, I screamed as he pinned my hands above my head with ease.

"Marcel bring me the zip ties." Up close, Victor was an imposing figure, broad shoulders, thick arms, chiseled jaw, and eyes the color of whiskey. Those eyes held no sympathy as he tightened the zip tie on my wrist, nor when he pinned my legs down so Marcel could do the same to my ankles.

"Do you think you can behave yourself when I get up?" Glaring up at him, I refused to answer.

"Yeah, I didn't think so. You know you could have made this much easier on yourself if you had just said yes to him. Now I'm forced to drag your ass back to him. Then I'll be forced to get rid of your body when he's had his fun with you. Do you know what that does to someone?" Victor spoke evenly to me as he got up, bent down, hoisted me over his shoulder and started walking. He acted all butthurt he'd have to dispose of my body, like it was my fault and not his fucked-up boss's fault.

"So, I'm supposed to feel bad because your psycho boss wants what he can't have? You understand how assbackwards that sounds right? Your boss couldn't take no for an answer, so he had to send his little goon squad to get me." My body bounced against Victor's massive shoulder as he continued to walk. Where the fuck was, he taking me? If he thought, I'd feel an ounce of sympathy for him he was sadly mistaken.

"Actually, I expected you to take his offer. Not many women resist him, you're a rare breed." Victor slid me down off his shoulder, leaning me against their car.

"Get the trunk opened. I'll be sad to see this body destroyed." Victor lightly caressed my cheek with a sad look in his eyes. I tried to jerk away from his touch.

"Poor fucking you, bet it hurts me more than it does you asshole." Victor grabbed the back of my neck, yanking me against him.

"You'd be surprised what hurts me doll." Wow cryptic much.

"Marcel, help me get her into the trunk." Marcel rushed to his side looking more than happy to help. Victor reached down for my legs while Marcel grabbed my arms, at least it was supposed to be my arms. Instead of my arms, he grabbed me by my tits.

"Hey asshole those aren't fucking handholds." Marcel just laughed, Victor growled, and I just prayed they didn't fucking drop me. Surprisingly, they are both gentle as they set me in the trunk, Victor even placed a blanket over me. This dude was really fucking confusing me; he was being semi-nice while simultaneously kidnapping me to hand over to his pyscho boss.

"What did the boss say, Marcel?" Victor ground out as they both stood by the open trunk.

"He said not to touch her, she was his. Remember that?" Fury clouded Victor's eyes, and Marcel took a step back.

"Oh, come on man, I barely touched her. It was just a little groping. What, you can touch her cheek, but I can't grab a little boob. What the fuck man?" Marcel took another step back, his hands out in a placating manner. In a flash, Victor pulled out his gun and shot Marcel in the chest. Marcel never stood a chance as he crumpled to the ground in a heap as I bit the inside of my cheek to keep from screaming. These fuckers were all psychos, and I was trapped with them.

Chapter Nine

HOLLAND

Getting to the cabin Crimson told us about felt like it was taking forever. What if Bella was already gone? What if Lorenzo's goons found her first? Too many fucking "what ifs" playing in my head. At least I had my crew backing me up, I didn't even have to ask for their help. Bart just called Pops and filled him before telling everyone to grab their gear and head out.

That's what brotherhood should be, dropping everything to help your brother in need. This was what I'd been searching for all along. I thought I needed to be a cop to get this kind of loyalty, but the truth was the club was there for me the whole time. They never turned their backs on me, even though for years we were on opposite sides of the law.

Family, brotherhood, loyalty, and devotion things I thought I'd get by joining the police force. Instead, I got rules, red tape, and regulations that kept my hands tied from doing what was right. I don't hate them anymore, I can't, they do a job within the rules of the game. They have a code they have to live by, but that's just not the life for me anymore. I'm a Reject now, it's probably where I belonged long ago, but I fought against this life.

I was like any rebellious teenager; I didn't want to be my father. Even though he's one of the best men I've ever known. He stepped up when my mom stepped out, dropping everything to take care of me and my sisters. But the Rejects were his life, and I rebelled against being a part of that life. Like the old saying goes though, the more things change the more they stay the same. Here I am riding up to a cabin, not in a patrol car, but instead cruising up on my Superglide behind Bart and Matt.

As soon as we cut the engines, I know something isn't right. It's too quiet, like that eerie quiet that happens in scary movies when something is about to happen quiet. Without a word, Matt motions for us to fan out. Our weapons are drawn, ready for anything, that's when the smell hits me. I knew that smell, being on the force I've had the unpleasant reality of smelling it more than once. Something or someone's body was near and decomposing.

When the body finally came into view, I let out a relieved breath of air, it wasn't Bella. It looked like the guy, whoever he was, had been dead for about a day at least. This meant if Lorenzo's goons had Bella, they weren't that far ahead of us. Just as I was coming around to the front of the cabin, Matt was exiting the cabin shaking his head.

"What's in there?" I started to make my way towards the door, but Matt stopped me.

"Nothing is in there man, just one destroyed cabin. It looks like she was hiding in a root cellar under the floorboards." I shove past him and take in the door barely hanging onto its hinges as the rest of the cabin comes into view. It looks like something out of a tornado movie, everything was upside down, broken, or in pieces. The hatch that led down to the root cellar was flung open, but there was no indication that there had been a struggle anywhere. That was either a good sign or a bad one.

"Holland!" Bart hollered from outside, and I rushed to his side. He was close to the wooded area looking down at the ground.

"What did you find?" When Bart looked at me, it was with concern in his eyes. I remember giving him a similar look when Bliss was found but didn't want to see him. He knew I felt something for this woman, even though we'd only met once. There was something about her that made me want to protect her and take care of her. Not that she needed it, because she was kind of a badass all on her own.

"It looks like there was a struggle of some kind over here. There isn't any blood, so they must have taken her alive. What about the body you found? Anything we can get from that?" Bart looked at me expectantly, hoping I had some good news.

"He's been dead about a day, maybe more maybe less. I'm not a coroner or medical examiner but based off of what I've seen before that's what it looks like. Which means they aren't that far ahead of us, but it also means our time is running out." Running my hand through my hair, I want to scream and rail with frustration. This reminded me too much of my sister's recent kidnapping and I didn't like it one bit. If what Crimson said was true, the guy who had Bella was much worse than the guys who had my sisters. This guy had power, money, and ruled with fear. If we went after her, it could cause problems for the Rejects. It could bring down the wrath of someone too big for them to handle.

"Stop. Just stop that thought whatever it was. We are doing this together. Even if you weren't a part of our club now, I'd still owe you for what you did for Bliss and Matt still owes you for what you did for Jesse. So we're in this, regardless of where it takes us." Bart pulled me in for a back slapping hug.

"Now call her sister and find out where the fuck they would take her, because I'm ready to fuck someone up already." Matt's "hell yeah" came from somewhere near the cabin followed by the rest of the guys. This is what it meant for someone to have your back no matter what and fuck me if it didn't feel pretty damn good.

Pulling out my cell, I dialed the clubhouse's number, that's where Crimson was staying. It was the safest place for her while we were out trying to find Bella. She wasn't happy about being left behind, but Bella sent her to me for a reason, to keep her safe, which was exactly what I was trying to do. Only thing was Crimson did not see things that way at all. I still had my doubts about whether she would stay put or not.

"Yo, this is Brick." It was Brickhouse, one of the newly patched members. Guy was built like a brick shithouse, hence the name.

"It's Holland, let me speak to Crimson." I can hear Brickhouse talking to someone with his hand over the receiver.

"She ain't here man." My heart stutters in my chest. She swore she'd stay put and of course she lied. I was going to throttle her. I can hear Brickhouse arguing with someone, but my mind is wrapping itself around the fact that Crimson is not where she's supposed to be.

"Chill out Holly, I'm here." It's Crimson and she's fucking laughing, I'm going to kill her.

"Thanks for the help Brick." If I could reach through the phone, I would.

"Don't ever do that again." I seethe through my teeth. Bart looks over at me like I've lost my mind and I shake my head in response.

"What the fuck was that shit Crimson? You know I'm out here looking for your sister and you want to pull fucking pranks." I hear her gasp on the other end; I've never spoken to her like this. Maybe it's because I'm wound like a fucking top, or maybe I thought we'd lost her like we lost Bella, I didn't fucking know.

"What the fuck man? She's crying. Crim, come on Crim I'm sure he didn't mean to yell at you. Seriously dude what the actual fuck!" Brickhouse is yelling at me through the phone while simultaneously trying to comfort Crimson.

"Come on babe, it's alright." Did he seriously just call her babe? I'm going to have to kill one of my own brothers at the rate this is going.

"Tell me you don't have your hands on her right now." I grit out, because she is too fucking young still to be messing around with bikers. Way to be a hypocrite Holland, my inner voice sneered.

"Never mind, I need to talk to her about her sister, put her back on." I'm at my breaking point with these two women.

"Not until you chill the fuck out dude." Brickhouse sounds pissed, but at this point, I give zero fucks if he's pissed or not. Taking a deep calming breath, I try to reason with him. We're wasting time that we could use to find Bella.

"Please explain to her it's about her sister, it's important." I could tell Brickhouse just to ask Crimson where she thought her sister might be taken to, but I was too pissed at the moment. Bella was god knew where and Crimson was playing fucking games, while probably flirting with Brickhouse.

"Babe, Holland says it's about your sister, he needs to talk to you about her. Come on, talk to him. Then me and you can chill for a little while together." Grinding my teeth, I try to remember that Crimson is now eighteen, she is no longer a child, and she's an adult who can make her own decisions. Even if they are horrible ones, that will lead to nothing but heartache; it is not my job to protect her from herself. I hear sniffling, which makes me feel like a dick, before her voice comes over the line.

"What's going on Holly? Did you find Bella?" There's still a part of me that wants to ream her ass for playing her stupid prank, but my need to find Bella is too strong.

"No we didn't find her, we found the cabin though." How much do I tell her? I decide not to give her all the gory details.

"She's not here and it looks like someone besides her was." I can hear her crying and Brickhouse asking if she's alright.

"Crimson I need you to focus. Where would they take her if they picked her up?" I know she's upset, but I need her to focus.

"I'm not sure. They got her, didn't they? I wasn't fast enough finding you. This is my fault isn't it?" I felt like an even bigger dick for getting angry with her.

"No it's not your fault, it's this asshole Lorenzo's fault for not being able to take no for an answer. Now think really hard was there anywhere your sister mentioned?" I can hear Brickhouse soothing her.

"Maybe this club he owns, it's in downtown Chicago, I don't know the name of it. But he shouldn't be that hard to find. Get her back Holland…please just get her back. Before he...before something happens to her." I know her fear; I know what Crimson herself has been through. Helping her and my sisters recover included me going to therapy sessions with them. I knew what they'd all lived through. Crimson was afraid that her sister was going to endure much worse, and frankly so was I.

"We'll find her, don't worry we will find her." I didn't add that I planned to make that fuckwad suffer for taking her in the first place.

"Holland man," Brickhouse came over the phone, "look if I'm stepping on toes here let me know and I'll back off. She said she wasn't with anyone." I can't help but laugh, of course he thinks I'm with Crimson, every fucking body thinks I've been with Crimson. It doesn't help that Crimson has taken every opportunity to make her interest in me known.

"Dude, she's like my sister. Fuck her over and I will end you, it's that simple." She knew what she deserved now, and I had to trust her to use that new knowledge just like she used her self-defense skills.

"I'm not trying to take advantage, just trying to keep her company. She's been upset since y'all left to find her sister and well…" He doesn't have to say anything else; he likes her. Whether that will last a night, a week, or forever, who the fuck knows.

"Like I said, you fuck her over and I will end you, it's that fucking simple man. I'll even have Matt and Bart help me do it. Otherwise, whatever happens is between two consenting adults, and I mean consenting dude not alcohol induced consenting either." We said our goodbyes and then I turned to the guys to fill them in. It was going to be like looking for a needle in a haystack and we were on a time crunch to find it.

Chapter Ten

BELLA

I hurt everywhere; my whole body feels like one giant bruise. Whether that's from being tackled to the ground or being stuck in this damn trunk for god only knows how long. I swear if we hit one more bump, I'm peeing, I can't hold it anymore. My bladder feels like I'm carrying the fucking ocean inside it. This cannot be good for my kidneys or my bladder, or fuck anything connected to them down there. Just when I think I can't take anymore the car rolls to a stop.

My anxiety starts to kick in, are we making a pit stop or is Lorenzo on the other side waiting for the trunk to pop open? I'm hoping it's a pit stop, I want to avoid Lorenzo for as long as possible. But then there's the other part of me, the one that's uncomfortable and in pain that just wants to get this whole shit show over with. Let him kill me and put me out of my misery. Muffled voices pierce the metal hull, but I can't make out who is talking or how many. My bladder is reminding me it's on its last string.

Kicking at the trunk I yell as loudly as I can, "I need to pee asshole!" Maybe I should have kept quiet, maybe I should have tried to make myself smaller, or whatever of the fuck damsels in distress do. But that's just not how I roll, I refuse to bow down to these assholes. I might be quaking in my boots on the inside, but on the outside, they will see nothing but raging bitch with no fear.

"Hold your fucking horses' woman. You in a hurry to die or something?" One of the other goons, not Victor, opens the trunk. Light flashes inside and I have to squint my eyes shut, it's so painful.

"No, you dick, I'm not in a hurry to die, but I sure the fuck would like to avoid pissing all over myself if I can help it before I die." I hear a low chuckle over to the side of the car, it sounds like Victor. Good, I'm so fucking glad I could make his sorry ass laugh. Dick!

"Elliot, help me get her out of there and I'll take her to do her business." Victor is there reaching for my legs as Elliot grabs me by my upper arms. They set me down and I barely keep from falling over with the restraints they have me in.

"Do you mind?" I lift my hands and motion toward my feet, trying to tell him I needed to be able to move. Instead of cutting me loose, he bent down and hefted me over his shoulder.

"What the fuck, put me down and untie me!" It does no good and being up on his shoulder is not doing any favors to my bladder at all.

"Shut up and enjoy the ride. Don't chicks like to be carried around?" Was he fucking kidding? Did he seriously think that women got excited about being carried by some psycho to pee?

"I'm clearly the exception to the rule." I huff out; this man is a quandary that's for sure. I'm not sure if he's genuinely trying to help me or if he's just an idiot controlled by Lorenzo.

"Clearly. Now hold still while I get the bathroom door open." He switches my position on his shoulder and I can hear a door squeak open.

"Ah here we go." He steps into the bathroom and sets me down, leaning me against the counter so I don't fall over.

"Yeah, here we go, but I can't go if you don't fucking untie me." Victor looks me up and down, like he can't understand why I can't just go. Are all men this dense or is it just Lorenzo's men? When he flips out his switch blade I jump, almost toppling over, but his arm catches me.

"I'm not going to cut you sweet Bella." He whispers against my ear. It's so soft it almost feels like a lover's caress, and it creeps me the fuck out. Victor is unpredictable and a wild card. He wasted his own guy because he touched me, while he's been touching me every chance he gets. I let out a sigh of relief when I heard the snick of the blade and my legs were loose. I'm still a bit wobbly, but at least I can now walk so he won't have an excuse to carry me.

"There that should make it easier. Here let me help you." My eyes go wide as he walks me over to the toilet sitting beside a beat up sink. I didn't get a chance to look around when they got me out of the car, but I'm pretty positive I'm not at Lorenzo's place yet. Lorenzo doesn't seem the type to live in anything but grandeur. No it looked like some kind of gas station bathroom or maybe roadside convenience store. The toilet was gross and looked like no one had cleaned it in a century or more, but at the moment I couldn't care less as long as I got to relieve myself. Victor positions me with the back of my legs to the toilet seat and then he's unbuttoning my pants. I squirm a little, because I don't want him or anyone else to see me naked.

"Relax Belladonna, I'm just going to help you." I swallow down the scream that wants to make its way up my gullet, refusing to show any more weakness to this asshole. Tilting my head up just a little, I tried to ignore his hands on my hips and the feel of his fingers grazing me as he pulled down my pants. I breathed through my nose, calming myself.

"I'm going to hold you up over the toilet. Wouldn't want that perfect ass of yours touching that seat." I feel his hands on my ass as he lowers me toward the seat. My bladder is screaming at this point and frankly I have no shame as I go. Victor's hands never wander, they stay there holding me securely while I finish my business. Victor lifts me until I'm standing and then grabs some paper towels from the dispenser and cleans me. My cheeks are probably red from embarrassment; no one has probably wiped my ass since I was a baby.

"There, now we can continue on our journey." Victor slowly pulls up my pants and buttons them as he stands gazing at me.

"Lorenzo is very happy we found you." Victory says grinning like a lunatic.

"Oh, goodie that means he'll be able to torture me soon. I can't wait," I deadpan. Victor clutches me to him, my body aligning against his very aroused one.

"If he breaks you, I'll put you back together sweet Belladonna." His lips brush against my cheek before he's pulling me towards the door. I have to swallow back the bile threatening to come up. The longer I'm with this guy the bolder he's getting.

"Yeah, I'm sure he'll just hand me over to you once he's done with me. Not like he's going to kill me or anything." I grit through clenched teeth. Doesn't he realize there won't be anything left for him to "put back together" once his boss gets a hold of me. Lorenzo is not known for letting anyone that crosses him live, and I've definitely crossed him.

"Don't worry, I'll be there to make sure he doesn't go too far with you. I can save you, just remember that." His fingers trail down my cheek, making me want to jerk away from his touch. I don't want to die, but I definitely don't want him to save me. That would be like going from the frying pan into the fire, no thank you, just kill me.

"Yeah, sure Victor, you can save me." Victor looks like he's going to say something else, but something has caught his attention over my head. I can hear what sounds like another car pulling up.

"Time to pay the piper babe, try not to anger him anymore than he already is. When he's angry it's worse." Victor suddenly flips me around with his hand around my waist, pulled close to his front.

"Remember what I said, only I can save you." He whispered close to my ear.

My nerves are getting to me, because I'm actually thinking of taking him up on his offer to save me. Satan is here, and as he steps out of the car, I can feel the anger radiating off of him. Lorenzo's eyes narrow as they take in Victor's possessive arm around my waist, but the fury in his gaze is laser focused on only one of us, me. My fight or flight instinct is working overtime, I need to run, but I can't.

Lorenzo stalks over to where we are standing, grabs me by my chin and turns my head from side to side. I know what I am to Lorenzo, nothing more than an object, and he wants to make sure his object is in working condition. When he nods to Victor to hand me over I can feel Victor's hesitancy, but he releases me anyway and then I find myself in Lorenzo's arms. I can feel every inch of his body and if he wasn't such a fucking douche, I might have been attracted to him. Sue me, the man smells like liquid sex, looks like sex on a stick, and is wearing one of those three-piece suit things that make girls stupid, including me. I never said he was ugly, just that he was a douche and a bit psychotic, big difference.

"Bella, Bella, Bella." Lorenzo says my name slowly while wrapping his arms around my body. To the outside world, it would look like he's being the courteous boyfriend holding his girl tightly. The truth is he's got a death grip on me, and it feels like my spleen might pop at any moment.

"You gave me quite the merry little chase didn't you." It's not a question, it's an observation, and on the inside, I'm jumping up and down with glee.

"Yeah, well some people can't take no for an answer. Do you know anyone like that Lorenzo?" I can hear his teeth grinding against each other and his lips have thinned into a straight line.

"What did you think was going to happen Lorenzo? Did you think you'd show up and I'd swoon at your presence? Not. Gonna. Happen. Whatever you take from me will be by force." His lips twist into a smirk, like he already knows this and finds it amusing.

"Oh Bella, I have so many fun things for us to try." He lifts me up over his shoulder and takes me to the car he came in. I expect to be put in the trunk again. Instead, he has one of his goons open the door and he places me on the soft leather seat before buckling me up. Victor slides into the front seat behind the wheel. He glances back giving me a wink, whatever the fuck that means. Meanwhile Lorenzo is giving orders to his other goons. I can't make out what he's saying, but his goons jump to it whatever it is.

"Behave for him Belladonna." Victor whispers right before Lorenzo climbs into the back seat with me. Lorenzo scoots over to the middle of the seat, wrapping his arm around me, giving me a squeeze like I'm his sweetheart or some shit. I'm surrounded by psychopaths, lovely.

Chapter Eleven

HOLLAND

"Are you shitting me?" Matt laughed beside me as we looked across the street at the Bianchi Bar. Yeah, so much for a needle in a haystack, all we had to do was look up bars in Chicago and there it was. Big bright lettering with flashing lights chasing around it.

"Damn, this guy's ego is bigger than yours bro!" Matt smacked Bart on the chest and he grunted.

"Fuck off asshole!" Bart punched Matt in the shoulder.

"My ego and dick are just the right size for all of this. Don't be jealous you didn't come equipped like I did." Bart ran his hand down his body like Vanna White showing off a brand-new car.

"Think we could just walk in there and ask them nicely to give her back?" Matt asked sarcastically. Bart and I rolled our eyes before turning to walk back to our hotel.

"Yep, let's just walk right in there and say, 'Mr. Bianchi, pretty please can I have my friend's sister back.' Pretty sure he'd kill us all before we got to finish that sentence." Finding the club was the easy part, getting Belladonna back was going to take a little finesse and maneuvering.

"We need eyes inside that club. What do you boys say about a little recon mission?" Matt slapped his hands together, rubbing them like he was eager to get started. Anything that promised a little action got him excited, and I had a feeling that there was definitely going to be some action happening during this rescue.

"Your mission should you choose to accept it is to infiltrate that club and get intel on where they are holding Belladonna." Bart spit out a laugh, and Matt was practically skipping down the sidewalk like a little kid eager for Trick or Treating on Halloween.

"Oh, I'm gonna accept that mission, and I'm going to get that intel quicker than either of you two losers. I can do this shit in my sleep, remember." It was one of the few times Matt ever mentioned his time in the service. He didn't like to talk about his time in, said there wasn't anything to talk about. Somehow, I got the feeling he was full of shit, especially when he said shit like he just did.

"Fine, fine. Whatever dude as long as we get the intel. It's not like being on the police force didn't teach me a thing or two about assessing a situation and gathering intel. As long as we get Belladonna back, I give zero fucks." We left the rest of our group at the hotel, wanting to be as inconspicuous as possible when we scoped out the club. As soon as we walked through our hotel room, the rest of the group started piling in.

"I say we split up, half our crew stays here waiting for a signal, the other half will go with us to the club. Leave your cuts here, if we get caught, we don't want this to blow back on the club. This asshole has connections and the less they know about us the better." Bart's plan made sense. I didn't want the club to be on Lorenzo's radar if this thing went sideways.

Over the next couple of hours whileas we waited for the club to open, we planned. First Matt and I would go in, hit the bar, check out the security detail. Then Bart would come in about thirty minutes later, followed by Tiny, Wrench, and Lugnut in thirty-minute increments. Reaper, Yankee, Bear, and Bull were to wait outside in the alley across the street for a signal if we needed help. I was hoping we wouldn't need to call them in, if we did that meant shit went sideways.

The club was definitely a hot spot in Chicago because the line to get in was halfway around the block by the time we walked up. There was no telling what was on the other side of that door, and the anticipation was killing me minute by minute. My adrenaline was pumping by the time me and Matty got to the front door of the club. The bouncer asked for our ID's, gave us a quick once over in our dark denim jeans and tight black t-shirts and ushered us in.

Music floated from the speakers set along the walls of the club. Not thumping bass, but more of a soulful R&B rhythm that was perfect for dancing. Matty and I wove our way through the crowd 'til we reached one of the many bars.

"Did you see that bouncer? Dude had to be like 350-360 easy." I nodded as I flagged down the bartender to get us some beers. We didn't plan on drinking much of them, but we wanted to blend in as much as possible.

"Yeah, his mother was probably part gorilla or something because he was jacked. I wouldn't want him coming to escort me out, that's for damn sure." After the bartender dropped off our beers, we both turned to scope out the place.

"Total of eight bouncers inside, four in uniform, four out. One at the door, two stationed near the DJ booth, and one by the restrooms all in uniforms. Then there is one at the end of this bar, pretending to drink his whiskey, one that's on the dance floor pretending to dance, and two sitting at the table by the hallway trying to act inconspicuous." Matty blended, swiveling his head to check out the bouncers and flirting with the women passing us in front us, seamlessly. It was scary how good he was at pinpointing where the enemy was, which made me wonder why he got out of the service.

"Alright let's make a trip around the room; Bart should be inside in about ten minutes. I want to get a peek at what's down that hallway over there. Think you can distract our two bouncers for a few seconds?" Matt made a noise in the back of his throat as if to say "seriously" before he sauntered off. He flipped me the bird as he walked backwards toward the dance floor.

I had no idea what his plan was until he went up to two women who were grinding against each other. From where I was standing it was clear they were already torqued and very interested in Matt. Their hands started to roam, but Matt subtly evaded their grasping touches while shaking his head. Then he bent his head in close to their ears before strutting back to where I was standing by the bar.

"Taken care of." He said dusting off his hands like he'd just completed a job.

"Dude you're a fucking genius, and if I was into guys, I'd kiss you right now. I was thinking maybe start a bar fight but getting those two to distract them is even better." Matt clutched his hand to chest like he was offended.

"Really I didn't earn a kiss Holly! I'm offended, I thought I'd at least get a peck from you." I shoved him away from me as he made kissy faces at me. People near us were chuckling and cheering him on.

"Knock it off dumbass we don't want to bring attention to ourselves. Remember to blend in, this is not blending in." I seethe through my teeth at him.

"Relax Holls, the best way to blend in is to be ourselves. The more we avoid interaction with those around us the more suspicious we look. Take my word for it, I've done this a few times." Matt flung his arm around my shoulders and steered me towards the bathrooms.

"Alright, I see your point. Where are we going? Aren't we waiting on Bart to get in here before we move?" Instead of answering me, Matt continues to drag me towards the bathroom hallway, swaying slightly.

"Man, I don't think I should have drunk that last beer." His words slurred as we passed the bouncer stationed at the bathroom hallway. I wanted to roll my eyes, but instead I pretended to hold him up, like a good friend would do.

"I told you, you can't hold your alcohol man, but you never listen." Once we're past the bouncer and inside the bathroom he pops up like a jack in the box.

"About damn time you two got in here." Bart's voice carries from a closed stall door. When had he gotten in the club?

"Yeah, well Einstein here wasn't getting with the program. Didn't you ever do undercover shit when you were on the force man? Blending in 101 is pretending to be like everyone else." I heard a toilet flush and Bart strolled out of the stall rolling his shoulders like he was preparing for a fight.

"No, I never did undercover. My face was too recognizable around town, and the only crime they were interested in busting was what was going on at your club. I wasn't likely to get that position, now was I?" I loved my friends, fuck they were my family, but sometimes I still felt like an outsider.

"Well, I can tell you this, Bella is here." Bart's declaration got our attention quick.

"Before I got through the door, I saw a car pull up down the alleyway, beside the club. I didn't get a good look, but I saw a guy with the same build as Lorenzo get out of the car. He looked like he was dragging a woman beside him. She wasn't using her legs so she's either drugged or knocked unconscious." She was here, in this building mere feet away from me, I mean us. Just the thought that she was helpless in their hands made me want to bust the whole fucking place up. But I knew we needed to play this right or all of us would be dead.

"We're not leaving without her." Both Matt and Bart nodded in agreement, but now we needed to figure out how to get her out without getting caught.

Chapter Twelve

BELLA

You ever have one of those hangovers where you remember what you did, but you don't remember how you got home. Yeah, well that's what happened, only I'm not home. No instead, I'm in sick twisted fucknugget's dungeon under his club or Lorenzo to everyone else. Like I remember being put in the car with him, I remember the drive across state lines, but how we got to the club, no fucking clue. My arms aren't working, my mouth is dry as a desert, and my tongue feels like sandpaper. Right now, I could probably sand someone's bureau for them with my fucking tongue and make them some cute shabby chic shit.

When I wake up, my head is pounding and I'm staring up at a concrete ceiling. I can hear the music wafting through, it's not very loud. I can tell it's his club, the same fucking club I turned him down in a month ago. I blink rapidly to adjust to the glaring lights on the ceiling. Listening closely, I don't hear anyone in the room with me.

My arms and hands aren't a hundred percent yet, but they help me get into the sitting position. Looking around the room, I see chains on the walls, shackles hanging from the ceiling in one corner, and what looks like wooden stocks. There was a drain set in the concrete where the floor sloped toward it. Surprise, surprise psycho asshole has a dungeon in the basement of his club. The couch I'm sitting on is plush soft leather, expensive shit, definitely not the knock off from IKEA.

There was a small hallway and when I craned my neck, I could make out the lines of a door. Briefly I wondered where my host was, but I pushed him out of my mind while I tried to get my legs to work. The chances of me actually making it out of this place alive were slim to none, but I wasn't going to go out without a fight. At least I knew Crimson was safe, Holland would take care of her. Crimson told me all about how he swooped in and saved her, she called him her hero. Holland would make sure she was safe, that Lorenzo and his goons couldn't get to her. If I didn't make it out alive at least I knew she would be okay.

My legs still felt like rubber and I knew I was running out of time. Lorenzo would be back any minute and I needed to use my time wisely. Sliding down the edge of the couch, I flipped over on my stomach. Using my hands and elbows, I crawled towards the door down the hallway. I sent up a little prayer that I'd make it to the door before Lorenzo showed up. The concrete floor tears at the skin on my elbows, I can feel the blood seeping from my wounds. My nails are nonexistent at this point. I've clawed them off making my way to the door; my fingers are a bloody mess. Just as I was almost to the door, the handle started to jiggle. I let loose a sob I'd been holding back, because I just knew this was the end for me.

"Ah Belladonna, my sweet why are you on the floor?" Victor steps through the door and stares down at me.

"Look at what a mess you've made." He makes a tsking sound as he lifts me off the ground and carries me back to the leather sofa.

"I was trying to get the fuck out Dodge." I wouldn't beg him to release me, I wouldn't beg any man for anything ever again. Begging my husband to stop hitting only resulting in being hit harder, it didn't take me long to figure that out.

"Oh, but Belladonna, if you leave then we won't ever be able to have some fun together." The gleam in his eye made me cringe a little inside. His idea of fun involved pain, mine involved me being anywhere but there.

"Lorenzo is attending to some business matters, but he'll be joining us soon. He already said I can have you when he's finished, isn't that generous of him." Victor reached over and caressed my cheek with the back of his hand.

"Yeah, very generous." I huff out in a sarcastic breath.

"So, fucking generous of him to just give a person to another person without their consent. Yeah, he's just a real fucking generous motherfucker ain't he." Victor's eyes narrowed at me; his lips thinned into an angry line. Then he must have caught himself because his lips turned up into a sinister smile as grabbed a handful of my hair, bending it back 'til I was looking up at him.

"You should have more respect for Lorenzo, beautiful Belladonna. Your sharp tongue can be removed if you're not careful." Victor pulled a switchblade out of his pocket and flicked it open running the dull end against my cheek. My body shivered in fear, I couldn't stop it from taking control. I knew he meant it too, Victor would cut out my tongue and smile while he did it.

"This would have been so much easier if you had just said yes to him. Now he will want to make you pay for insulting him. He can be very creative in his punishments, bringing you so close to the edge of death without going over." Victor has a glazed look over his eyes, like he's remembering some torture scene from the past.

All I can do is try to remain calm when what I really want to do is run screaming from the place. It's like he views Lorenzo as some fucking God to worship, nothing like running into a fanatic for human beings and their sick perversions. Suddenly the door down the hallway bursts open and there's a bunch of guys pouring in yelling at each other.

"I'm telling you the bathroom is this way!" One guy slurred as his buddy grabbed him to keep him standing up. That's when I saw Holland. He'd changed, instead of the clean-cut police office he looked like he belonged in a punk rock band. His hair was a shocking blue that was shaved on the sides to make it a Mohawk. The tight black tee he was wearing showed every dip and valley on his body along with the tattoos on both of his arms. I had to stop myself from humming in appreciation, because he didn't look like the safe cop anymore. No, he looked downright dangerous, and his fury was aimed right at Victor.

"Hey, you can't be back here." Victor jumped up waving his hands at the group of guys trying to push them back out the door. I was dumbstruck, unable to even formulate words. Was Holland here for me? But why would he come for me?

"Hey man chill, we're just trying to find the bathroom." A good-looking guy with sleeves of tattoos said to Victor right before another guy clocked him in the jaw, knocking him out. Holland rushed over to where I was sitting on the couch, kneeling in front of me taking in my bloody elbows and fingers.

"Fuck Bella, are you alright." He let out a harsh whisper, like he was afraid he'd spook me. The other two guys pulled out guns. One aiming directly at Victor and the other aimed at the door down the hallway.

"I'm fine, now get me the fuck out of here please and thank you." Next thing I knew his arms were under my body and he was carrying me towards the door. If it wasn't for the fact that I was pretty sure my legs still weren't working, I'd give him shit for treating me like a damsel in distress.

"Holly, what are we doing with this asshole?" I glanced over Holland's back to see one of the guys with his booted foot on Victor's back.

"End him Matty, end him now. He's lucky we don't have more time." Holland seethed through clenched teeth.

"Right on man, I got you." I barely registered the softened sound of the gun going off as we made it to the door. Victor was gone, done, fineato. Now if we could only get rid of Lorenzo my life might be able to go back to normal.

Matty and the other man followed behind us as we made our way through the door and started up a set stairs. At the top of the stairs, Holland shifted my weight so he could open a door. I expected light to flood us, but instead it's pitch black. The music from the club is much louder now, we must be getting closer to the actual club portion of the building.

"Where are we?" I whisper to Holland, still a little shocked that he came for me. He barely knows me. Why would he come for me? Not that I'm complaining at the moment, but it still doesn't make sense to me.

"We're not sure exactly, it looks like it could be a storage area, but there's nothing in here. We're going to get you out of here, there's an exit just a few feet away. It's probably how they brought you into the club when you got here." I nod even though I'm sure with the darkness he can't see me.

"Come on before Lorenzo remembers he has a plaything waiting on him. The sooner we are out of this place the sooner I can be back in the arms of my woman. No offense Bella." The tall guy I hadn't gotten a name for said quietly. I cringe a little thinking about how I'm the plaything he's referring to.

"She's not a fucking plaything Bart, shut your fucking pie hole." Holland growls out as I do a little happy dance inside at the fact that Holland doesn't see me as a plaything. It's the little things that make me happy.

We slowly made our way toward the exit Holland mentioned. Matt eased the door open as quietly as possible, none of them sure how far the sound would travel. Once we were all out, Matt closed it behind us just as quietly. As soon as the door was shut, Holland started running down the alley behind the club. I bit my cheek to keep from screaming out in pain every time my elbow made contact with his body. There was no way in hell I was going to be the reason we didn't get away.

None of us talked as we ran; we all knew what was at stake if Lorenzo or his men caught up to us. Holland didn't slow until we were in the parking lot of a hotel. He made his way around the back entrance, Matt and Bart following closely behind us. I thought Holland would put me down any minute, but he held me tightly against him. His body was warm against mine, giving me ideas that it shouldn't. Even bloodied and half-drugged my body responded to his nearness. What the fuck was wrong with me? I can't be right in the head if being near a hot guy minutes after escaping psycho assholes is making me horny.

Chapter Thirteen

HOLLAND

I don't want to put her down, she feels too fucking perfect against my body. Like she was made for me. What the fuck is wrong with me? This woman clearly had been put through hell, she was bleeding, and I was having thoughts of her lying naked under me with my cock buried deep inside her. Instead of keeping her in my arms, I lowered her to the bed as gently as possible.

"I'm not made of glass dumbass it will take more than what those assholes did to me to break me." Bella smiled to lessen the sting of her reprisal. I looked over her obvious wounds checking her fingernails which looked like they'd been put through a meat grinder and her elbows didn't look much better.

"Chill, I got those while trying to escape. Crawled across the concrete floor, made it all the way to the door before dick for brains came through the door. I was this close to escaping on my own, even with two legs that didn't want to work." Damn she was one tough woman, she didn't wait around to be rescued, she rescued herself. That shit was sexy as fuck.

"Holly, we need to get out of here as soon as possible. Sorry sugar but how long until you can ride?" Matt was right we needed to get out of there, but I had a feeling her legs still weren't working completely. I was ready to tell him we'd wait 'til she was ready when she spoke up.

"Don't be sorry, I want to get the fuck out here as soon as possible. My legs are starting to get feeling back, I'm not sure how long it will take for them to be a hundred percent though. I'm even willing to forego a shower and a clothes change if it means we can book it out of here sooner." I smiled down at her squeezing her shoulder.

"Good as soon as your legs are operational, we're out of here. I don't know if anyone saw us at the club or if Lorenzo has surveillance cameras anywhere. Didn't see any, but better safe than sorry. I'll get the rest of the guys ready to roll out as soon as you give us the signal." We both nodded at Bart in response as he and Matt walked out the door. Which left me and Bella alone together in a hotel room, with a king size bed. The things that were running through my head that I wanted to do to her needed to be shut down. She'd just been through some traumatic shit; she didn't need some asshole she barely knew lusting after her.

"Are you hungry? I can run down to the vending machine and grab you something." I didn't really want to leave her alone in the room, but I also wanted to take care of her; there was something about her that called to all my protective instincts.

"NO! Don't leave me." She flung her hands out as if to stop me.

"Shit, that sounded pathetic didn't it." I grabbed the office chair from the tiny desk in the corner and sat down in front of her.

"Look Belladonna, you've been through some scary shit. No one will fault you for being scared, not me, not Bart, and definitely not Matt. Both of their women had shit happen to them, I won't go into detail, but they know sometimes you just need time to heal. And well my sisters went through some shit that changed them both." Her head was bent down, and she was plucking nonexistent lint on her shirt.

"Please call me Bella, creepo Vincent called me Belladonna." Her voice sounded so small. I wanted the girl who was full of fire back.

"Is Vincent the guy that was with you? Did he work for Lorenzo?" I didn't want to say that Matt killed, but we both knew who I was talking about. If she was calling him a creepo chances were he'd hurt her or tried to hurt her. Damn if that didn't make me want to raise him from the dead so I could kill him again.

"Yeah, he was psycho number one in Lorenzo's little army of goons. Told me after Lorenzo was through with me, I was all his. Said my name like it was a prayer, creepy as fuck." She still kept her head bent while she talked; I could tell she wasn't used to talking like this to someone. I had a feeling that she didn't let many people see her vulnerable, and right now she was definitely feeling vulnerable.

"Well, his ass ain't getting you or anyone else for that matter." That brought a small smile to her lips, her very kissable lips. Damn it why couldn't I think about her without my dick getting involved.

"Fuck yeah, I hope he rots in fucking hell." Some of her spirit seemed to come back.

"He killed one of the other guys, Marcel, for touching my boobs. The way he talked about Lorenzo was like a religious fanatic, creepy as fuck." It sounded like we'd gotten to her in time, but until she told me herself, I'd proceed with caution.

"That must have been the guy we found at the cabin. Crimson told us where to start looking for you. When you weren't there, and we found the body we figured you'd been taken. She told us about Lorenzo's club being in downtown Chicago but didn't know the name. Luckily the asshole has an ego the size of California and named the club after himself." I shook my head at the thought. Lorenzo was sloppy which meant he had people covering for him. I was pretty sure the guy who did all the covering for him was dead in the basement of his club. It worried me a little because if no one was there to clean up Lorenzo's messes and keep him under control then he was even more dangerous to us. There was no way I was going to bring that up to either Bella or the guys though. No sense in causing undo panic if we got out of there without being seen.

"I'm glad Crimson had you, she hasn't had a lot of people she can count on. She thinks of you like an older brother, okay a hot older brother." Shaking my head because I knew how Crimson felt, or at least how she felt before I left her at the clubhouse. Bliss and Jesse would take care of her, make sure she stayed out of trouble; at least I hoped they would. If the phone call with Brickhouse was any indication, then they probably weren't doing such a good job.

"Yeah, she's a good kid. Who is hopefully staying out of trouble while I'm away. Do you want to call her?" I reached for my phone, but Bella put her hand out to stop me.

"No, let's wait 'til we are far away from here. The less she knows the safer she is. Lorenzo knows I have a sister; I wouldn't put it past him to use her to get to me. We have to keep her safe. Do you understand? Crimson's safety is your priority. I can take care of myself, and I can handle a hell of a lot more than she can." Bella took a shaky breath before continuing.

"She deserves to be happy; to go to college, to meet boys, to date, to get married. She deserves all that shit and if something happens to me you need to make sure that happens. Do that shit for me or I'll chop your balls off and feed them to you. You got me?" Tears were on the edges of her lashes, and her voice cracked just a little. This woman amazed me; instead of worrying about her own life, she was worrying about her sister.

"I got you, but Bella she's just as adamant about making sure you're safe you realize that don't you. If I save her at the cost of you, she'll never forgive me. So how about we both agree to keeping you both safe so I can keep my balls right where they are. I kind of like where they are and want to keep them there as long as possible." That earned me a bigger smile and little laughter.

"Fine, keep your balls if you must. I think my legs are coming back to life. No idea what the fuck they gave me, but whatever it is this shit doesn't like to wear off, probably some kind of horse tranquilizer. Isn't that what the mob uses?" She laughed as she spun her body to the edge of the bed, placing her feet on the floor. I reached out to help her stand and was rewarded with a glare.

"Hey, I'm just trying to keep you from falling. We need to get out of here. Remember? Let me help you. Scout's honor I won't tell anyone you needed help." I did some kind of symbol with my fingers hoping she would believe I'd been in the scouts. Judging by her pirate eye squint and the shaking of her head, I'm going to say it didn't work. But she didn't push me away and let me help her stand up.

"Alright they seem to be holding me up alright; no swaying and I can feel my feet. Now let's take a few walks around the room to get this blood flowing again." Leaning on my arm, her breasts squished between us, she started walking around the room with me. The longer we walked the less she needed to lean on me. When we'd made a whole circuit around the room without her needing to lean against me, she did a little happy dance.

"That's right baby I'm back, time to get the hell out of Dodge, or in this case Chicago." Her smile spread across her face lighting up her eyes. I had the urge to kiss her; she was so damn tempting.

"Wow if you're this excited about walking, I bet riding on the back of my bike really gets you going." Bella froze and looked at me.

"Ride? With you? On the back of your bike? Didn't anyone bring a car? A truck? A plane maybe?" She looked upset at the prospect of riding with me.

"No, I'm sorry we all brought our bikes. It was faster to travel that way. If you don't want to ride with me there are a couple of guys with us, you could ride with." There was something deep in my gut screaming at me not to let her ride with anyone else, but I had to tamp that shit down. She wasn't the kind of woman who took well to feeling like she was owned. I didn't want to own her, I wanted to give her the freedom she'd lacked for so long, while at the same keeping her entirely to myself. Okay so I'm a greedy bastard; sue me.

"It's just that...I haven't ridden on the back of someone else's bike in a long time. Last time I road bitch was when my husband was alive. Swore I'd never ride bitch again." Her arms were crossed giving me that look like she was ready to fight me over this.

"Don't think of it as riding bitch, think of it as the road to freedom with me as the driver." She didn't look convinced.

"If there was any other way to get you back home, I'd do it, I'm sorry." I didn't want her uncomfortable, but at the same time she didn't have the option of being picky right now either. Finally, she relaxed her stance a little.

"Fuck, fine I'll ride with you. Let's get this fucking shit show on the road. The next stop I need a shower, food, and some sleep." I saluted her like she was in charge and we left the hotel room to join the others. It was time to go the fuck home, and fast.

Chapter Fourteen

BELLA

Sitting behind Holland, feeling the heat of his body against mine, brings back memories of our night together. He looks different, and smells different, but he feels exactly the same. There's a reason I snuck out while he was sleeping, I didn't want to leave. He felt like home to me, and that was dangerous. I swore I'd never let another man have control over me, and Holland had the power to break me in ways Cain never could.

Cain broke me mentally, Holland could break me emotionally, and there was no way I was letting that happen. Especially now that he's in the Hades Rejects, those guys weren't known for being cute and cuddly bikers by any means. If the rumors were true, they had blood on their hands, and lots of it. They were lethal and took retribution for any slight against their club. No, staying away from them sounded like a great plan.

Before his death, Cain's club had the same reputation. They would retaliate against anyone for anything they saw as an insult. Whoever the person was who wronged the club had to pay for the insult with blood. Sometimes it was just beating them up, other times it was a bullet in the head. Cain used to say if a man didn't have the respect of those around him, he at least needed to have their fear. Because fear is what makes people obey you. Something he taught me very early on in our marriage. I wouldn't go back to living like that again, not even for Holland.

I'd let him and his little band of merry men take me to Crimson. Right now, I was safer with them then on my own and I had no way of getting to Crimson without their help. I didn't like feeling like I owed them. Luckily, my good sense overruled my guilt over owing them for my rescue. Lorenzo would be looking for me and being with the Hades Rejects pretty much guaranteed he wouldn't fuck with me currently. The question was after I left the safety of their club what would happen. I needed a plan to keep me and Crimson safe, while avoiding anything else to do with the Rejects in the process.

Before long, we were pulling into a motel parking lot. It didn't look like much, but it did look clean and well maintained. Hopefully that meant no bugs and fresh sheets. Honestly, I just wanted a shower and some sleep. It felt like I'd been in a boxing match, all my joints and muscles ached. Between being in the trunk of Victor's car and whatever Lorenzo gave me, I was like one giant bruised body. A long soak in a hot bath would do wonders for my achy body.

Holland held his hand out to help me slide off his bike. Good to see he didn't lose his manners when he put on that Reject's patch. I had to admit he made one helluva profile in his leathers with his hair spiked and his shades on. He was wearing a muscle shirt so I could see the definition in his arms with his tattoos flashing in the waning light of the sun.

"Like what you see beautiful?" He smirked, catching me staring at his ink.

"Just wondering what happened to you. When I left you were a clean-cut cop, now you're…" I wave my hand to encompass his whole body and the bike he's still sitting on.

"Things Bella, things happened." There was a pain-laced note to his voice, which only made me curiouser to find out what happened. Whatever hurt him enough to turn his back on being a police officer must have been pretty fucking bad. I clenched my fists ready to battle whatever or whoever had caused him pain.

"Calm down hellcat, no need to ruffle your feathers." I narrowed my eyes at him.

"Your thoughts are just like Crimson's; they're written all over your face. There's nothing you can do now to change the way things happened. I'll explain later, once we get you home and we can talk." At the mention of Crimson, I smile thinking about how right on the money he is. Crimson couldn't hide her feelings if you paid her to, they were always written right there for everyone to see.

"Home, what home? I don't have a home to go to these days." Holland sighed and ran his hand over his Mohawk like he was frustrated with me or something.

"We'll talk when we get to my place. How about that?" Crossing my arms over my chest, I tapped my foot and stared at him.

"Don't do that Bella, this is not a discussion we can have while on the road. There's too much to say and not enough time to say it the right way." I was just about to demand he tell me everything when Bart came back to the bikes with room keys.

"Alright double up and get some shuteye." He handed Holland a key card, gave me a wink and then headed over to where Matt was standing.

"He doesn't seriously expect you and me to share a room. Does he?" Holland just shrugged while he rummaged through his saddlebags before turning back to me. I stomped off toward the front desk, determined to get my own room when Holland's arms circled my waist, pulling me against him.

"Where do you think you're going?" He asked barely above a whisper against my ear, sending chills down my spine.

"I'm going to get me a room, put me down." I said turning around in his arms.

"With what money sugar?" Shit.

"I thought so. Come on there are two beds and we both need some sleep after traveling so long." I couldn't be alone with him in a room with a bed. I'd never make it through the night without being tempted to jump his bones again. Fuck my life.

"Fine." I huffed out as I followed behind him to our room; I made a mental note to deball his buddy for sticking us together. Not that I'd want to share a room with any of his little biker buddies, but at least then I could avoid being alone with Holland. Of course, his buddy thought we were together or some shit.

So now I'm stuck in a room, alone with the man who fucked me six degrees 'til Sunday not that long ago. A man, given half a chance, I'd climb again just to feel a little of what he had to give. Walking away from him the morning after was the hardest thing I've done in my life. I needed to get my head on straight, I needed to pull my girl panties on, make sure they stayed on, and woman up. He came after me because of Crimson, not because he cared about me.

Stepping through the motel room door I took in the cheap, but clean bedspreads. They looked like something out of a seventies porn all brown and patchwork quilt looking. It smelled like bleach and pine cleaner inside, and upon inspection of the bathroom, the tiles shined like diamonds in the light. It wasn't fancy, but whoever owned the place definitely took care of it.

"I call dibs on the shower." I yelled as I made a mad dash inside the bathroom sticking my tongue out at Holland. His deep laughter could be heard through the door.

"Hey, I have some clothes for you to change into if you want them." He sounded a bit unsure of himself.

"It's not much." I crack the bathroom door so I can look at him. The uncertain look on his face says he's ready for me to reject whatever he has for me.

"At this point I'd take a pair of your boxers and a dirty t-shirt." I tossed my old clothes outside the door.

"Those are filthy, and not just because I've been wearing them for a few days." They were filthy because other men touched me while I wore them. Holland seemed to understand what I meant and held out his hand with his offering in them.

"My sisters...my sisters when they...the first thing they did was shower and want clean clothes." What the hell was he talking about? His sisters? Now I was all confused.

"I'll explain after you get out. But it's just some simple leggings, new under things that Crimson helped me get, and a comfortable shirt. I got some warm fuzzy socks when you come out you can have too." My heart stuttered for a second at the sweetness of this man before me. Hardass cop turned big bad biker, was a softy and it made me melt a little.

"Thank you." I said softly as I closed the bathroom door and leaned against it letting out a sigh. Oh Holland, just when I think I've got you figured out you go and surprise me.

I take the longest shower probably in history, scrubbing every inch of my body twice. The water is running cold by the time I get out. There's a part of me that feels guilty for hogging all the hot water, but I push that down. My nails look better now that they are clean. It was just the tips of a few that had small cuts from the rough concrete of the floor. My knees hurt like a bitch now that I could feel them. I made sure to clean them thoroughly too, which meant breaking the scabs. Pulling on the clothes Holland gave me, I threw open the bathroom door like a queen exiting her throne room.

"Boom baby!" Yes, I'm the woman who loves the Emperor's New Groove, sue me. Holland was laying back on the bed closest to the door, with his hands behind his back smiling at me. His eyes raked over my body, sending tingles up my spine making my nipples stand at attention. Calm down, he's just a hot man who gave you orgasms. You can and must resist him.

"One pair of warm fuzzy socks." He smirked at me holding up a cute pair of socks with hearts all over them. They definitely looked warm and comfy, but I hesitated going near him. I was pretty sure my willpower would not hold up if I got too close now that I was clean. Fuck my life.

"Come on I won't bite, well not unless you want me to." I blinked at him; I wasn't afraid of him I was afraid of what I would do if I got close to him. It was hard enough being on the back of his bike smelling his scent, feeling his muscles bunching under his jacket. He let out a heavy sigh and tossed the socks on the other bed, my bed.

"I get it, you don't want to be near me. I'm going to grab a shower. Wrench is outside standing watch while I do, but if you need me just holler." He raked his hand through his hair, let out another heavy sigh as he made his way to the bathroom, closing the door behind him. I flopped back onto the bed and stared at the ceiling letting out my own sigh. Oh Holland, if you only knew how much I do want you near me.

Chapter Fifteen

HOLLAND

After a very cold shower, because my beautiful roommate used up all the hot water, I was able to finally get my raging hardon under control. Bella pushed all my buttons, my protective buttons, and my caveman wanting to claim woman buttons. When she'd come out of the bathroom being all cute, I had to grip the bed to keep from sweeping her into my arms. It was clear she didn't want me, the night we spent together was her way of thanking me nothing more.

By the time I exited the bathroom she's out cold, curled up under the blankets clutching a pillow. A part of me was slightly jealous of that pillow. When I glanced over at my bed, I noticed the pillows were moved around and I whipped my head back to Bella. Had she taken my pillow to snuggle up to? Shaking my head, I made my way to the door so I could let Wrench know he could leave. I slowly cracked open the door to look outside, trying not to make any noise, Wrench lifted his eyebrow at me.

"I'm out, thanks man." He nodded and headed towards his door.

"No problem, she's a fine piece that one is. Better lock it down before someone else moves in." I narrowed my eyes at him, and he put his hands up to placate me.

"Not me man, but some of the other guys were checking her out is all I'm saying." He said nervously.

"It's not like that with us, she's Crimson's sister. Tell the others anyone fucks with her and they'll answer to me." I cracked my knuckles anticipating the fight. Wrench shook his head walking away. Quietly shutting the door, I leaned against it to help calm me down.

If anyone of those assholes thought, they were going to try and get my woman they were wrong. Shit, my woman, she wasn't anyone's woman. From what I could tell she planned on staying that way too. There was no locking it down like Wrench said. She didn't want to be locked down, especially not by me. I groaned as I looked up at the ceiling hoping for guidance, there's none there.

Glancing over at Bella she's beautiful, breathtaking the way her hair fans out around her, her thick lashes lay against her cheeks, and her plump lips slightly pouty. When she's awake, she's all sass and mouth and I love it. Hell, I crave it from her. But when she's asleep it's like she's transformed into some fairy or nymph, she's just that beautiful. She doesn't want me though; she's made that clear. Fuck my life.

I turn off all the lights, double check the door locks, and look outside one last time to make sure no one is out there. There's this feeling something is about to happen racing through me, but I don't know what. Placing my gun on the table beside the bed, I strip down to my boxers and crawl into bed. Hopefully, I can get some sleep before we have to be up and going again tomorrow. Having Bella sitting behind me is like having a shot of adrenaline constantly flowing through me. I was wired, every touch, every move she made my body felt it all and responded.

Later I wake up with a start looking around the room, unsure of what woke me up. I'm usually a hard sleeper, not much wakes me up once I'm asleep. That's how Bella and Crimson snuck out of the house last time. My head swivels to her form, and I notice she's shifting back and forth like she can't get comfortable. She moans and flings her hand up like she's punching the air. Suddenly she's screaming while throwing punches into thin air.

Logically I know she's dreaming, and I can't do anything but wake her up. The illogical part of my brain wants to slay whatever demons she's fighting. Flinging the blankets off, I rush to her side touching her face. Her breathing started to even out, my name, a whisper on her lips. Was she dreaming about me? About us?

"Bella. Bella, wake up. You're dreaming sweetheart, wake up." I shake her shoulder just a little, hoping that will work to wake her up. They dream has a hold on her, she's locked tightly in its grip, it's going to take more than a little shake to wake her up.

Sitting down on her bed, I pulled her into my arms, too late I noticed she's in nothing but her shirt and panties. She still hasn't woken up; her arms are flailing around, and she clocks me before I can stop her. I grunt in pain as she catches me on the cheek, not hard enough to do any damage, but enough that I'll feel it in the morning.

"Come on Bella, baby wake up." I push her hair out of her face and run a finger down her cheek. Even with a scowl on her face, even though she just tried to lay me out, she's still the most beautiful woman I've ever seen. Leaning down I place a small kiss on her lips, more like a whisper of a kiss, but it works. Her eyes flutter open, and they get as big as saucers as they take me in.

"What the fuck are you doing? Why am I in your arms?" Sass and mouth is back at it already, not even seconds awake. I can't help but smile down at her perturbed face.

"You were having a dream. I tried waking you up gently but that didn't work. So I decided to kiss sleeping beauty and it worked." I cocked my head to the side, smiling at her, like I haven't a care in the world.

"Well, I'm awake you can put me down now." She looks at everything else but me, like she's afraid to meet my eyes. I'm not holding her tight; she could get up any time she wanted, but she wants me to put her down, that wasn't happening. Shaking my head, I ran my fingers through her hair, I remember she liked it when I touched her hair.

"Nope, you want down, you get down on your own sweet cheeks." I don't know why I'm baiting her, but I can't help myself. Something deep down tells me she's not as immune to me as she acts all the time. I'd bet money she enjoyed being with me just as much as I enjoyed being with her. Her pulse quickens and her breath hitches as she finally looks into my eyes. What I see in the depths of her eyes makes me groan.

"We shouldn't do this again." She says as she straddles my thighs, and maybe she's right, but at the moment I don't give a shit.

"This is a bad idea; tell me this is a bad idea Holland." She pleads with me. I shake my head no, because as far as I'm concerned this is a great fucking idea. There might be regrets in the morning, but right here at this moment I have zero. I want her, she wants me, nothing else matters.

Wrapping my hand around the back of her neck, I pull her lips to mine kissing her with all the pent-up feelings I have for her. If I can't tell her how I feel, at least I can show her, make her feel it. She moves her hips in sync with my kisses, slowly rubbing her panty covered core against me.

"Fuck Bella I've missed this." Pushing me onto my back she shimmies down my body grabbing the waistband of my boxers. I lift up a little to help her slide them down as she reaches for my rock-hard cock licking the tip.

"Mmmm...I've missed this too." She grins up at me like the cat that got the canary as her mouth descends on my cock, swallowing it whole.

"Holy fucking hell Bella!" I gasp out, not sure how much longer I can handle her wicked tongue as she starts to bob up and down on me.

"Problem Holland?" She asks as she pops off my dick smiling. Instead of responding, I yank her into my lap and grind my erection against her soaked panties. Flinging her head, she moans in satisfaction rotating her hips.

Running my hands up her sides, I lift the shirt off her body; her lush breasts bounce just a little causing me to zero in on her nipples. Light and dusky they beckon me to them, like a siren's song. Latching onto one nipple, I nibble and suck, lavishing it with attention before moving onto the other one. All the while she is using me like her own person fuck toy, rubbing her panty-clad pussy against my throbbing cock.

I can't wait any longer, I reach down to the string on the panties and rip them off of her. She lets out a shocked gasp but goes right back to grinding against my length. I can tell she's close, but I want in that pussy when she comes, I want to feel those walls strangle me and send me over the edge. Flipping her over onto her back, she looks up at me with desire in her eyes.

"Please." She whispers as I rub against her opening, she's soaking wet for me. "Please Holland." I can't say no to this woman, even if I wanted to.

As I slide into her warmth, our groans mingle with each other. We fit so perfectly together, like two pieces of a jigsaw puzzle. I know at that moment I can't ever give her up, she's mine. There's just a tiny problem of making her see that before she bolts again. Sliding slowly in and out of her, I watch her breathing start to become erratic. Her nails grip my back, the pain only adds to the experience.

"Fuck baby you're so tight. I could stay here forever." Her eyes shutter at my words, forever isn't something she wants to hear. Too fucking bad, I'd prove to her it wasn't a bad word. I'd make it my mission to show her every fucking day for the rest of her life it wasn't a bad word. All I've done since she walked out on me was think of her, wanted her, and now that I had her in my arms again, I never wanted to let her go.

"Forever baby, say it for me." I changed my angle just a little until I was hitting the spot that made her back arch. It was a dirty move, but I wasn't averse to playing dirty to get what I wanted.

"Say it." I ground out.

"Forever." Smiling at her response, she gritted out through her teeth I picked up speed. Slamming into her over and over again, rocking the bed into the wall. Whoever was on the other side of that wall was probably pissed.

"That's right baby. You're mine. Mine, forever." She nodded her fingers digging into my back. I could feel her fluttering around my cock, she was close, and I wasn't far behind her.

"Fuck Holland, fuck." When she exploded, it was like a rocket went off, her whole body felt like it tightened around me.

"Mine." Slam.

"Mine." Slam.

"Fucking mine!" I roared as my orgasm took over my body holding her hips to keep me from falling over. Staying seated inside her, as the aftershocks shook us both just kissing her gently, I knew what we'd just done was life changing. She clung to me, running her fingers along my back and arms, like she couldn't stop touching me. I had zero complaints as I rolled over and curled into her body.

Chapter Sixteen

BELLA

Waking up next to Holland two things were quickly apparent. One, even in sleep he was sexy as fuck. His face relaxed and a slight smile played on his lips. I imagine I'm responsible for this smile ghosting his lips. The second thing, the thing that I've tried to avoid since meeting him; I had feelings for him. I swore off love, it wasn't something I could let into my life again, but something had shifted with Holland. Cain took my love and beat it to death until it was nothing but a bloody pulp. Holland had the ability to destroy me completely.

My first instinct was to run, get as far away from him as fast as I could and not look back. He was a prospect for a MC, and not just any MC, but the fucking Hades Rejects. But were they really as bad as everyone claimed they were?

Crimson told me about how they were the ones who took down the prostitution ring that she'd been in. Then they came with Holland to rescue me, someone who wasn't even affiliated with their club.

"You look wound up tight as a long-tailed cat in a room full of rocking chairs." Holland startled me out of my musings smiling over at me.

"Good morning to you too handsome." I smirked over at him. Why did he have to look so damn good first thing in the morning? I was pretty sure I looked like something a cat coughed up.

"Yes, good morning beautiful." His voice got all husky as he turned toward me kissing me gently on the lips. My heart did a little fluttering thing, damn it.

"Now tell me what's got your panties in a wad first thing this morning after such an epically orgasmic night." I couldn't help the snort of laughter that came out.

"Epically orgasmic? Is that what you're calling it?" I shook my head smiling, enjoying our early morning banter. Something I'd never had a guy do with me before. I usually feigned sleep when Cain got out of bed just in case, he woke up angry. A little more of my defense against Holland crumbled away.

"Yes, that's exactly what we are calling it and I plan on having it with you again soon." He stretched showing off his sculpted body, giving me a knowing smile. Like he could tell I was admiring all those muscles he had one display.

"You want to tell me what had your forehead all scrunch up and that pout on your lips or should I take a guess?" He didn't sound mad, but there was a definite seriousness to his tone. I fidgeted a little with the blanket wrapped around my chest. There were questions I needed answers to, but what if I didn't like the answers. Fuck it, if there was one thing, I'd learned from dealing with Lorenzo it was tomorrow was not promised.

"It's the Hades Rejects." I let that statement sit between us for a minute. Holland reached over and pulled me into his arms, his chin resting on top of my head.

"Ah...that's a long story, but I'll tell it to you." He told me about the struggles he faced while trying to stay within the law. How staying within the law probably prevented them from finding Bliss sooner, he held a lot of guilt for what happened to her. But the Rejects were the ones who got Bliss her justice. Then he explained how when Jesse killed a man in self-defense instead of thanking her, the police investigated her. He talked about how the last straw was when their hands were tied when trying to find his sisters. The Rejects stepped up and helped him not only find them, but exact retribution.

It didn't sound like the Rejects just killed people to kill them, not that he admitted they killed anyone. But I knew what he meant by retribution and justice for those women. They sounded more like vigilantes righting the wrongs that the cops couldn't or wouldn't. Maybe I'd been wrong about them.

"So, you're saying they are misunderstood heroes?" I wasn't completely picking up what he was putting down, but I wanted to believe he wasn't involved with people like Cain. Yeah, it was shitty to think guilt by association, but if you hung out with guys like that you tended to pick up some of their bad habits. I couldn't afford a repeat, no matter what my feelings for Holland were.

"No, definitely not heroes. More like The Red Hood from Batman. They dish out justice with no regrets. I won't lie to you, they don't work within the spectrum of the law and it bothers me sometimes, but they don't hurt anyone who doesn't have it coming. They've always been there for me, even when I couldn't be there for them." Holland twirled a piece of my hair with his fingers before reaching his hand behind my neck and bringing our lips together in a scorching kiss.

"Damn, what is it about you Bella? When you're around all I want to do is touch you. It's like there are magnets inside us pulling us together. Tell me I'm not the only one feeling this shit." He touched our foreheads together, cupping my cheek. I leaned into his touch like I'd done it a hundred times before. It felt so fucking natural with him, like I didn't have to put out any effort. I could just be with him.

"You aren't the only one. Fuck." I sighed as he kissed me softly.

"I can't do this Holland. I can't." I tried to stand, but he held onto my arm.

"What can't you do Bella?" His eyes searched my face, for what I don't know, but his expression changed to one of aloofness and ease.

"You can't do me? Because, sweet cheeks you already have, twice." He released my hand when I glared down at him, his words cutting deep.

"Ah, there he is, the real you. Here I thought you were talking about some kind of real connection. Instead, it must have just been your dick finding that homing beacon in my pussy again." Grabbing at my clothes to put them on, I turned away from him to hide the pain. I didn't see him coming. He had me picked up, tossed on the bed, and himself planted between my legs before I knew what was happening.

"You can't do this?" He slid into me in one stroke.

"Hmmm? Tell me Bella." When he was inside me everything else disappeared. All my worries, all my past, everything was gone but him. But he couldn't stay inside me forever.

"I can't be what you want me to be." I couldn't be his old lady, couldn't go back to that life again.

"What do you think I want you to be?" His cock glided out before slamming back in, my back arched. Forcing my brain to focus was becoming harder.

"I want you, nothing more, nothing less. I want all this sass and ass." He grabbed my ass and flipped me over onto my hands and knees like I weighed nothing.

"Every." Slam.

"Last." Slam.

"Bit." Slam.

"Of." Slam.

"You." My body melted into him, begging for more, as he hit all the buttons on me like I was fucking slot machine.

"You want a woman who will sit at home waiting for you to come back to her." I panted out.

"That's not me." I slammed back against him, determined to take a little control, but he wouldn't let me. He grabbed my hips to keep me from moving as he started slow thrusts, driving me crazy.

"See, that right there is exactly what I'm talking about. I don't want you sitting at home, I want you beside me." He ran his hand down my back in a soft caress.

"I want you to be my ride or die baby." His lips gently kissed my spine, tears formed in my eyes from the tenderness I felt from him. No one had ever been like this with me, and that scared the shit out of me. Flipping me back over, he bent over me until our foreheads touched kissing me softly.

Something inside me clicked into place, like a missing piece to my puzzle. His scent, his touch, the feel of his body wrapped around mine, all made me feel like I was home. There was something about him that gave me a sense of peace, a sense of belonging, something I'd never felt before. I ignored the voice inside my head that told me to run. He had the ability to destroy me, I knew this and yet I also knew I needed him. I didn't need him to survive or to keep me safe, no I needed the man he was, nothing more.

"You have the power to destroy me." I whispered.

"Don't." He smiled down at me, slowly stroking in and out of me. His hand wrapped around the back of my head, his eyes never leaving mine, keeping us connected.

"I won't my beautiful Bella, I won't." He whispered against my lips as he claimed them and I believed him. His thrusts became more urgent, his thumb flicked against my tiny button. Before I knew what was happening my back was arching, my toes were curling, and I was screaming my release. Holland roared out his own a few seconds later, collapsing on top of me.

"Now that is how we should wake up every damn morning." He smiled down at me before his lips met mine. Banging on our door made us both jump, Holland reached for his gun sitting on the table beside the bed.

"Kickstands up in fifteen…move your ass Holly." Holland groaned into my neck.

"I'm going to fucking kill Matt one of these days." I giggled.

"Hey, it's not funny he's trying to make that my road name, that shit is not cute. Don't be smirking at me Miss Sassypants." He poked me in the ribs making me laugh even harder.

"You heard the man Holly, kickstands up in fifteen." I shoved him off of me and made a mad dash towards the bathroom. He caught up to me and we spent the next thirty minutes in the shower not worrying about leaving. I could definitely get used to waking up every morning just like this with him.

By the time, we came out all the guys were standing by their bikes smirking at us. I gave zero fucks what they thought, I was fucking happy for once in my life. This time when I climbed on the back of his bike, I did it as his woman, a smile playing on my lips. I was his, he was mine, and we'd stand together in the face of whatever came our way.

Epilogue

HOLLAND

One Year Later

Sometimes in life you get a chance at something great, not good, but fucking great. Bella was my chance at something great, and over the last year I've shown her how she means to me every damn day. I won't say everything has gone smoothly, because that would be a lie. Bella is as prickly as a cactus some days, her own fears get to her, but I make sure to remain solid for her.

Somehow Lorenzo is in jail for murdering his buddy Victor. Someone called in a tip to the local police and they found him, along with the gun used that night at the club. When they searched the rest of the club, they found drugs and a room full of women chained to the walls. All fingers pointed directly at Lorenzo and he went away for a very long time. It reminded me that sometimes the law does work on your side, even if you have to give it a little hand in the right direction.

The day he was convicted Bella threw a huge party at the clubhouse and sold off all of Cain's property. It gave her a nice little nest egg to live off of until she decides what she wants to do. Crimson is in college working towards her Associate's Degree in graphic design. She's been dating Brickhouse for the past year, and he's planning to ask her to marry him once she graduates. He asked for mine and Bella's blessing, and we both agreed as long as he waited 'til she was at least finished with her degree.

Standing in front of all my friends and family, I totally understand his need to claim her. That's why after six months of living with each other I asked Bella to marry me. It took her another three months to say yes. Damn I loved her sass. Once she said yes, I wanted to make it official as soon as possible. So here we are in the field behind our cabin getting ready to say our vows.

Looking around at my family and friends I see how happy they all are. Even my sisters are here with Matt's brothers. I'm still not thrilled at the fact that we might become family for real because of those four but seeing my sisters happy again makes up for it.

"You nervous?" Bart asks from beside me.

"Nope, not one bit. This feels too right to me to be nervous." Bart gave me a knowing smile as he looked over at his own woman Bliss holding their daughter.

"Yeah, I understand completely. Here she comes." Glancing up the small aisle, I saw my woman making her way slowly towards me. She took my breath away in her lace dress, that swayed a little as she walked. Spaghetti straps held up the lacey confection, with layers of lace for the skirt part that came up at an angle to show off her legs. Her hair was pulled back by a single clip attached to her small veil.

"Breath babe." She whispered up at me with a smile playing on her lips. Life couldn't get any better than that moment as we said the words that would make us one. When the preacher told me to kiss the bride, I picked her up and crushed my mouth against her. Whoops and hollering commenced as I made her mine forever.

The End